THE WORLD'S FINEST ASSASSIN

Gets Reincarnated in Another World as an Aristocrat

† Maha

The proxy representative of Lugh's cosmetics brand. She provides logistical support by collecting funds, information, and more.

† Naoise

The oldest son of House Gephis, one of the four major dukedoms. He is a handsome boy brimming with talent and has a penchant for hard work.

† Tarte

Lugh's personal retainer and his assassination assistant. She cares deeply for Lugh because he saved her life.

† Dia

A noble lady from a foreign country. She is among the strongest mages in the world.

† Lugh

The oldest son of the clan of assassins, who is often called a boy genius. He was the world's greatest assassin in his previous life, and he combines that knowledge with the magic of his new world.

† Epona

The hero. The strongest person in the land, but suffers from anxiety and a lack of self-confidence.

Contents

The World's Finest Assassin
Gets Reincarnated in Another World as an Aristocrat

Aiming twenty rifles at once would've been impossible for an ordinary mage, but Limitless Growth made it no problem for me.

THE WORLD'S FINEST ASSASSIN

Gets Reincarnated in Another World as an Aristocrat

2

Rui Tsukiyo

Illustration by Reia

YEN ON

New York

The World's Finest Assassin Gets Reincarnated in Another World as an Aristocrat, Vol. 2
Rui Tsukiyo

Translation by Luke Hutton
Cover art by Reia

SEKAI SAIKO NO ANSATSUSHA, ISEKAI KIZOKU NI TENSEI SURU Vol. 2
©Rui Tsukiyo, Reia 2019
First published in Japan in 2019 by KADOKAWA CORPORATION, Tokyo.
English translation rights arranged with KADOKAWA CORPORATION, Tokyo through TUTTLE-MORI AGENCY, INC., Tokyo.

English translation © 2021 by Yen Press, LLC

Yen On
150 West 30th Street, 19th Floor
New York, NY 10001

Visit us at yenpress.com
facebook.com/yenpress
twitter.com/yenpress
yenpress.tumblr.com
instagram.com/yenpress

First Yen On Edition: April 2021

Yen On is an imprint of Yen Press, LLC.
The Yen On name and logo are trademarks of Yen Press, LLC.

The publisher is not responsible for websites (or their content)
that are not owned by the publisher.

Library of Congress Cataloging-in-Publication Data
Names: Tsukiyo, Rui, author. | Reia, 1990– illustrator.
Title: The world's finest assassin gets reincarnated in another world / Rui Tsukiyo ; illustration by Reia.
Other titles: Sekai saikou no ansatsusha, isekai kizoku ni tensei suru. English
Description: First Yen On edition. | New York : Yen On, 2020–
Identifiers: LCCN 2020043584 | ISBN 9781975312411 (v. 1 ; trade paperback) |
    ISBN 9781975312435 (v. 2 ; trade paperback)
Subjects: LCSH: Assassins—Fiction. | GSAFD: Fantasy fiction.
Classification: LCC PL876.S858 S4513 2020 | DDC 895.6/36—dc23
LC record available at https://lccn.loc.gov/2020043584

ISBNs: 978-1-9753-1243-5 (paperback)
        978-1-9753-1244-2 (ebook)

10 9 8 7 6 5 4 3 2 1

LSC-C

Printed in the United States of America

I woke up when morning arrived. I felt something warm on my left arm and turned to face it.

"No, my lord, shtoooop iiit…"

Tarte was hugging my arm and talking in her sleep.

Tarte was fourteen years old, had soft blond hair, and possessed a developed figure for her age. When she was younger, she had been abandoned by her family and left for dead in the mountains. The resulting trauma gave her occasional anxiety attacks. When it became too much for her to bear, I allowed her to sleep with me.

It's well known that the warmth of another person can give you a sense of ease.

"What in the world is she dreaming about?"

Looking at Tarte's happy sleeping face put me in a good mood.

Lately, we'd been sharing the same bed more often. I was worried that Tarte wasn't doing well mentally, but then I realized she was just making excuses to spend more time with me. I should've chided her, but I didn't see much harm in it.

She's doing her very best for me, and she worked exceptionally hard yesterday. I can let her have this.

"Tarte, wake up."

I pushed aside the temptation to watch her sleeping face and shook her shoulders. If she didn't awaken soon, she'd be late preparing breakfast.

Tarte's eyes lazily flitted open. She released my left arm and sat up.

"My lord, I love you shooo muuuch...," she said in a slurred voice as she leaned over to hug me.

I couldn't help but recognize her well-developed body through her thin nightgown. She nuzzled her cheeks into my chest as I attempted to move away.

"I know you love me, but would you mind letting go?"

"Come ooooon, it'sh fine. What'sh thish compared to what we did earlier...?"

"I don't know what you're referring to."

"It was like a dream, you— Owww!"

I pinched Tarte's cheek, and her eyes teared up.

"Tarte, it's time to wake up!"

"Wh-what—huh? W-was that just a dream?"

"Good morning, Tarte."

"Ah, uhhhhhh, my lord, that was, um... Eeeek!"

Tarte flushed deep red, pulled away, and rolled over until she fell out of bed.

Evidently, Tarte thought she'd done something quite embarrassing.

"Um, that wasn't what it looked like. I was just..."

"Don't worry about it. You were still half-asleep. But forget about that—look at the time."

"...Ah, I need to hurry!"

Tarte's face went from crimson to pale. She opened my closet and took out her servant clothes. I turned my back to her, and she began to change. Tarte had started storing some of her clothes in my closet after we began using the same bed.

"O-okay, I'll go make breakfast! I'll apologize for what I did this morning later, my lord!" Rotating back around, I saw that Tarte was now dressed in her maid outfit. After bowing, she beat a hasty retreat.

"This is the first time Tarte has had that much trouble getting up."

Usually, she was a morning person. Perhaps all the excitement the other day had left her exhausted. She'd really pushed herself to help me on my quest to save Dia. During my absence, she'd refused to sleep.

I wasn't tired, but that wasn't to say I didn't experience my own sort of problem.

"Man, the reasoning and bodily instincts of a young man truly can turn you into a different creature altogether."

I sighed. Being hugged by Tarte during the height of puberty while she was wearing a thin nightgown was poison. The sexual appetite of the fourteen-year-old was not to be underestimated.

My body had a habit of responding prominently, and I could feel that desire welling up inside me right now.

…*I'm her teacher, and I'm like a father and an older brother to her. I need to be more careful.*

I headed for the living room at the usual time. My parents and Dia were already at the table when I walked in.

"Good morning, Lugh. Look, I gave Dia my old clothes. Don't they look good on her?"

"They look lovely. White suits you, Dia."

Dia was wearing a thin, alabaster summer dress. It matched her white skin and silver hair excellently.

"Thanks, but I feel a little embarrassed wearing this. It's been a while since I've worn something so girly."

"Hmm-hmm-hmm, I knew my clothes would be a perfect fit for you, Dia. Tarte's a little too short, but it's her large chest that really makes her a difficult dress-up doll... *Ahem*. It's too bad I can't play with her, too."

"Don't you make clothes, Mother? You enjoy making revealing clothing, as I recall," Dia remarked.

"Making clothes from scratch requires a lot of trial and error! You're much easier. I can put you in any of my old outfits that I want!"

My mom liked Tarte and had recently been sewing different accoutrements for her.

"Hey, Lugh. Who is Tarte?" Dia asked with a stiff expression.

"She's my retainer, apprentice, and assistant. She shows real talent and has a strong work ethic. When I came to save you, she did everything she could to help. Speak of the devil, here she is."

Tarte walked in from the kitchen to set the table. She started by giving everyone their drinks. Today we had freshly blended apple juice.

"This is Tarte," I announced.

"Ah, that's right, you two haven't met yet. Tarte, introduce yourself to Dia," instructed my dad.

"O-okay. I am Lord Lugh's adherent. My name is Tarte."

"I'm Dia; nice to meet you. And thanks."

"I-it was nothing. I only did what was expected of me as his retainer."

"Hmm, you like Lugh, don't you?"

"Huh? N-no, I really respect him, and I love him, but not

in that way," Tarte quickly stammered out, clearly flustered. Dia remained composed.

"You don't have to hide it from me. Lugh is a nobleman, after all. Having a few mistresses is to be expected." Dia, being a noble, understood that sort of thing well.

A single wife was a risky choice for an aristocrat. If that woman couldn't produce an heir, the lineage would die out. Even if a child was born, there was no guarantee they would live to see adulthood. Among the gentry, having multiple wives and heirs was just common sense.

"Th-that's not necessary. Being by my lord's side is enough for me."

"You must care deeply for him. Lugh is a lucky guy, being adored by such a cute girl," Dia said.

"Not a day goes by that I'm not thankful for Tarte," I admitted.

"Huh?! I-I'll get the food. Excuse me!" Tarte blushed and ran back to the kitchen.

Dia's brow furrowed as she watched the other girl leave. After a moment, she turned to face my dad.

"Cian and Lugh, thank you for lending House Viekone the power of House Tuatha Dé. I'm afraid I was brought here with naught but the clothes on my back, so this is all I can offer. I hope it will suffice."

Dia extended a hand toward my dad. Sitting atop her palm was a ring fitted with a large gem.

…Dia talked the gift down, but the ring looked like it could've been a national treasure. Selling it surely would've earned you enough money that you, your children, and your grandchildren never would've had to work a day in your lives. That little thing was the epitome of priceless.

"We can't accept this. It's a memento from your mother, right? You don't need to give us anything. Count Viekone has already done enough for me. Also, Lugh is the one who acted, not I. He says he was just fulfilling a promise he had made to you," my dad replied.

"I understand. Perhaps you'll accept it as a payment for my lessons, then?" Dia once again offered the invaluable band.

"What do you mean?" asked my dad.

"Please teach me how to be an assassin. I need the knowledge of House Tuatha Dé. I'm great at magic, but I know now that's not enough. So please."

All the recent trouble at Dia's family estate had probably forced her to realize her own helplessness. As the daughter of a count, Dia did receive basic combat training. That wasn't enough for her anymore, though. She wanted the skills and knowledge only the Tuatha Dé clan of assassins was privy to. Undoubtedly, she hoped to help her father. The man had been forced into hiding as he built up strength.

"The skills of the Tuatha Dé clan are usually only entrusted to direct descendants. I see no problem making something of an exception, however. You're being made my daughter, after all. Let's talk about this after breakfast. The soup our adorable retainer is making for us is going to go cold."

As if on command, Tarte brought bowls into the room. She'd made fish soup, and its delicious smell wafted toward us as she set our dishes on the table.

"I second that," I added. "I want to enjoy Tarte's delicious cooking to the fullest."

"Okay. We'll save the matter for after our meal," Dia agreed.

We planned to finish breakfast, and then my dad would talk

with Dia about becoming my little sister. Once that was settled, we'd handle everything else.

Five years ago, in the Alvanian Kingdom, a new experiment had begun. It aimed to bring together young mages all across the country to foster friendship and competition. One of the reasons Dia was being made my little sister was to go with me to that place.

Tarte finished setting the table and stationed herself behind me as she always did. I'm sure she wanted to eat with us, but that would've set a bad example for the other servants.

Our breakfast entrée was dried fish soup made of catches from a lake in our domain.

"Lugh, I've never seen this kind of fish. What's it called?"

"It's Runamass. It's tasty, filling, and a common dish here in Tuatha Dé."

"It smells so good," Dia admired as she stared at the liquid and the large slices of meat.

"Let's eat. Words cannot accurately portray a dish's taste."

"Yeah, you're right. I'm excited to try it!"

Dia and I both sampled some of Tarte's cooking.

It was exceptional, but that was to be expected of Tarte. The broth was filled with ample portions of fish and vegetables. In true Tuatha Dé style, she'd added a small amount of lemon juice to bring out the flavor. This dish was originally a specialty of Mom's, and she'd taught it to Tarte.

In addition to the soup, we also enjoyed bread topped with goat butter.

It, too, was marvelous. The soy bread had been made with leftover sediment extracted from the soybeans used in Tuatha Dé to create emulsifiers, which were then sold to my Natural You cosmetics brand. Not only was a loaf tasty, but it was also good for you.

Since apples were in season, we drank their juice.

The day's morning meal had been made entirely using ingredients from the Tuatha Dé domain, showing how great our food could be. I enjoyed the sumptuous dishes of the capital, but I fancied the modest cuisine of Tuatha Dé more.

"It's delicious and simple. All the food here is," Dia complimented.

"That's the kind of domain Tuatha Dé is. That's exactly why I like it," I answered. "We live in harmony with the earth, and we're a prosperous domain in the truest sense. There is no better example of that than our cuisine."

As we neared the end of our meal, my dad spoke up, saying, "Now that we've all had our fill, let's talk about the future. Continuing to live as Dia Viekone is going to be difficult."

"Yeah, I understand that. I'm a fugitive, after all," Dia remarked.

"For that reason, I have prepared a new name and identity in the family register for you. You will be Claudia Tuatha Dé, Lugh's little sister."

"What?! But I'm sixteen years old! It doesn't make any sense for me to be Lugh's little sister."

"I know that you're older, but it's the only identity I have prepared on the family register. It wouldn't be impossible for me to make a new one, but...identities made without proper preparation are easily exposed. I prepared the Claudia identity on the family register fourteen years ago. I doubt anyone would be able to discover it's fake."

That younger sibling character had been prepared as insurance in case a particular situation came to pass.

"But won't people find it weird if I say I'm fourteen? It's sure to sound suspicious," Dia muttered, not on board with this proposal. Mom put a hand on her shoulder.

"It'll be fine. You're short, you're still baby-faced, and even your chest is tiny. Heck, I think twelve would work!"

"...That wording hurts my feelings. Also, I don't want to hear that from someone over forty who looks like they're in their twenties!"

"Youthful features run in the Viekone family. But it's not such a bad thing. When you reach my age, your friends' skin will dry, and they'll begin to sag in various places, but that's not something we have to worry about!"

It was a fairly convincing argument, especially coming from my mom. As someone who looked half her age, she was living proof. Just like her, Dia would probably never age. In a way, my mom's youth was a mystery deeper than magic.

"I'm still growing! I'm taller than I was last year, and my chest has gotten bigger, too!" Dia protested.

"Hmm-hmm-hmm, I wouldn't get your hopes up. I felt the same way...," my mom replied with an air of experience. Evidently, she understood where Dia was coming from.

"*Ahem.* Can we return to the topic at hand?" Dad cleared his throat to regain everyone's attention.

My mom's appearance had actually caused trouble for my dad as well. They elicited quite a bit of gossip whenever they went to parties or other social functions. People would regularly say he was too old for her.

"There is one more reason you need to be fourteen. In the

Alvanian Kingdom, all mages are made to attend a royal academy for knights from the summer of their fourteenth year to that of their sixteenth year. Attendance is compulsory for nobles, and commoner mages are welcome to attend through an application."

"The Alvanian Kingdom's Royal Knights Academy? I've heard of it."

The school must have been famous if Dia had heard of it. Until yesterday, she hadn't been living in the Alvanian Kingdom.

"That's right. As you know, the strength of an army depends on how many spellcasters it has. But just having mana alone isn't enough to make one useful in battle. For that reason, the young mages in this country are trained in the art of war to be called upon in times of emergency. That's the purported purpose of the academy anyway."

None doubted the power of mages. Just by enveloping themselves in mana, they rendered the swords and arrows from ordinary soldiers completely trivial, and they gained enough strength to cleave through an armored person with a single stroke.

Untrained amateurs were incapable of employing that incredible power to its fullest. That's why all mages now spent two years training.

Because the Alvanian Kingdom maintained only a small standing army and relied on its nobles for almost all of its military strength in times of emergency, having capable magic users was very important.

"Do you mean to say there's another reason for the academy?" Dia inquired.

"That's right. The nobles in Alvan have a strong sense of independence. Many don't even see themselves as subjects of the kingdom. They view themselves as kings of their own little countries. That sort of mindset creates closed-minded people. The kingdom wants to use the school to expand the worldviews of young members of the aristocracy. Interacting with other nobles their own age should instill them with a greater sense of scope and loyalty to Alvan they would not otherwise have. My generation may have forgotten where its allegiances lie, but the next generation will not."

I think it was mainly for the second reason that this system was introduced five years ago.

"Ah, so that's why nobles are forced to comply, while commoners are not. The reason my being sixteen would look bad is that people would think I skipped out on the mandatory attendance," reasoned Dia.

"Correct. If you are fourteen, you'll be able to go to the academy this year. I want you to go to study with Lugh next month."

My dad failed to mention that the hero had also recently been discovered. They were the same age as me and had similarly been born a noble. Whoever they were, they would be attending the academy. It was the perfect chance to get close and ingratiate myself with them as a school friend.

These next two years would be the perfect opportunity for me to study the hero as much as I wanted. Assassinating them was sure to be a cinch if I could get close to them.

"Okay. I'll be Lugh's younger sister. It's a little unfortunate, though... I wanted to marry Lugh someday."

As Dia smiled sadly, my dad tilted his head in confusion. "Why would being brother and sister make you give up on marriage?"

"Huh? Isn't that obvious? Because we're siblings. They can't get married."

"What are you saying? That's normal in Alvan," commented my mom, also appearing confused.

Guess I need to fill Dia in.

"Dia, in the Alvanian Kingdom, producing mages is the first priority. Suppose both parents are not mages. Then the odds of their child having mana decrease. Aristocrats surely possess the means to search for a suitable partner, but if they can't find one, they can pay a member of a lesser noble family for the service of helping to produce a child. Sometimes even that option isn't available, however. In such a case, a noble may have no choice but to make do with a relative," I explained.

"Huh?! You're saying people spend money to have children?! And by 'make do with a relative,' do you mean siblings?!" Dia exclaimed.

"Yeah, that's why marriage between family members is allowed in Alvan."

Dia's face flickered between a deep shade of red and ghostly white. "I'm glad I can marry Lugh, but it may take a bit to sort out how I feel about this," she admitted.

"We're not closely related by blood, so it should be fine. It's not as if we need to tell people we're relatives when we go out."

Dia went silent for a bit.

"Okay, fine! I won't worry about it. But don't expect me to refer to you as my older brother!"

"Even though you've always made me call you my big sister?"

"I've got two years on you, so that one makes sense! Also, you can keep calling me that."

I felt like we were acting a little careless. If Dia was okay with it, however, then that was all that mattered.

My dad nodded in satisfaction. "So from now on, Dia is

Lugh's little sister and my daughter. You're welcome to call me Papa if you want."

"Ooh, you can call me Mama, too! I've always wanted a daughter!" my mother chimed in.

"No way. That's too weird," Dia answered, immediately shooting that idea down.

From that moment forward, Dia was my younger sister.

"Lugh will teach you our clan's ways of assassination. As a direct descendant of House Tuatha Dé, you are entitled to that knowledge. I'd feel uneasy about conducting your training myself since you leave for the academy in only a month. With Lugh as your instructor, though, you can continue your lessons at school."

"Understood. I'll take responsibility for instilling Dia with the knowledge of our clan," I stated.

I'd already been thinking about how to guide Dia. We were going to be a team from then on, after all.

…Also, the boys at the academy were going to have about as much control over their sexual appetites as monkeys. I intended to safeguard Dia from their evil influences, but there was a small chance she could get into a situation where she'd have to protect herself. Training her would equip her with the necessary tools to ensure her own safety.

"Uh, Lugh, you're scaring me a bit with that face."

"I was thinking about your practice regimen. You have nothing to worry about. I promise to help make you stronger."

"Don't go too hard on me."

"I'll be careful not to overwork you."

I vowed to get her ready without pushing her too far.

We had one month before we'd go to the academy. That intervening time was going to be spent on a lot more than just assassination practice. The most pressing was that Dia, Tarte, and I needed to do some shopping.

The three of us were going to be heading to Milteu to make some essential purchases. Everything we required could be found there. I had a few matters to tend to as Illig as well.

We were traveling to Milteu by carriage. The journey would typically take a few days. That was far too long for my liking, so I made use of a few tricks to speed us up and cut the trip down to a single day.

"I can't believe how fast we're going. Everyone we pass looks at us in shock."

"I'm using a little bit of medical magic. I cast some spells to increase the horse's physical ability and stamina recovery. I'm also changing the horse every time we stop in a town. There's no limit to what one can do with money and magic," I declared.

"...Sometimes it's hard to believe you're human, Lugh. Ah, I almost forgot. Let's go on a date once we get there." Tarte looked on in jealousy as Dia snuggled up against me.

Conveniently, "Dia" works as a nickname for my new little sister "Claudia."

"If you're fine with it mostly being shopping, then yeah, let's make it a date. We're going to Milteu to buy things we need for the Royal Academy. You read the letter, right?"

"I did. I'm not sure what the purpose of some of these items is, though," Dia admitted as she took out the list.

The school had sent a similar missive to every fourteen-year-old noble mage.

It included a permit for entry into the Royal Academy and a list of things we needed to bring with us.

"Um, Lord Lugh. Would it be okay if I went to the academy with you?"

"Of course. I need you, Tarte. I want you at my side."

"...I'm pleased to hear it. I'll do my best!"

Common folk could apply to attend the academy so long as they had mana. Aristocratic students were also permitted to bring a retainer with them. Those servants were even allowed to take classes with their lords or ladies. Tarte was in a unique position to apply as either a commoner mage or a servant, but the latter afforded her more flexibility, so we went with that.

"Whoa, so this is how Lugh picks up girls," Dia remarked.

"...I didn't mean it that way," I shot back.

"I'm not angry. It makes me proud to see you do so well with the ladies."

Our carriage continued to move with incredible speed. I prayed for nothing to go wrong in Milteu.

We arrived in the city ahead of schedule.

It was the first time I'd come as Lugh. During my two years here, I'd lived as Illig Balor of the Balor Company. Walking the streets, I passed many people I recognized, but none of them noticed me. It was a funny feeling.

"Let's look at athletic wear first, since tailoring will probably take a few hours." I was talking to Dia, but when I turned around, she wasn't there. Tarte laughed. She raised a finger to point where the other girl had ventured off to and led me there.

"Lugh, what's this?" Dia asked, entranced by the sweets being sold at a food cart. She looked cute as she drooled.

The trolley was carrying baked bread made from dough filled with honey and various flavors of jam. The smell wafting from the cart was sweet and pleasant.

"This is a popular sweet in Milteu, called barta. You pick the jam you want when you order. They're delicious."

"I have to try one… There are so many jams, I don't know which one to pick… All right, I've decided. I'll go with loquat jam."

"What kind of filling would you like, Tarte?"

"Um, I like apricot."

"Excuse me, sir, can we please have one blueberry, one loquat, and one apricot?"

"Coming right up. Look at you, young man. How'd you end up on a date with two beauties?"

"Jealous, right?" I said, grinning jokingly.

"You bet I am. I'm so jealous I'm gonna do this!" While laughing merrily, he gave us all a large serving of jam on our bartas.

It was kind of him to treat us, and I tipped him accordingly. Once they were ready, I handed Dia and Tarte their sweets.

"Thanks, Lugh. Wow, this is good!"

"Sorry for pressuring you into getting me one, my lord."

"No need to worry. These are cheap, and I was hungry, too."

I bit into my barta.

Not only was the honey-filled dough sweet, but it was moist as well. In contrast, the jam had a refreshing tartness that made it seem less sugary. It kept the taste from being overpowering.

The jam was even spread onto our bread in the shape of each of our chosen flavors.

You could see many food carts selling bartas throughout Milteu, but very few were as good as this one. My merchant's instinct was telling me to entrust this man with a full store.

Maybe I'll mention that to Balor next time we meet.

"This is delicious! It looked like a lot of food, but it's not very filling, so I think I'll be able to finish it no problem," said Dia.

"I'm surprised, too. I want to know how to make this jam. This is so much better than the kind I make. It's a little frustrating," admitted Tarte.

"This is probably the best barta in Milteu," I remarked.

"Hey, Lugh, can I try a bite of your blueberry one? It looks really good," requested Dia.

"If we're trading, let me in, too!" Tarte insisted.

We all traded bites of our pastries. The loquat and apricot ones didn't disappoint, either.

Admittedly, sharing food with Dia and Tarte gave me a greater sense of happiness than any treat did.

When I looked up, I realized the three of us had attracted a lot of attention from the people around us.

Eating with two beautiful girls evidently attracted a lot of wandering eyes. The staring was starting to feel uncomfortable, and I decided we'd better leave.

After we finished eating, we went shopping and perused some street vendors. I spent two years working in this city for the Balor Company, so I knew the popular stores pretty well.

We bought only the highest-quality products. Cheaping out on tools would only come back to bite us later.

"The tailor should have our clothes finished by evening," I said.

"Sounds good. We were able to buy better stuff than I expected," Dia replied.

"I do like what we've purchased today, but when it comes to ease of movement, my usual clothes are better," Tarte added.

She was talking about her assassin outfit. The academy's list made it clear that a student could bring anything to use as athletic wear, so long as it was easy to move in. Unfortunately, those assassin outfits were made using the secrets of House Tuatha Dé. Wearing such a secret material in public wasn't allowed.

"Those Tuatha Dé clothes are functional and comfortable, but they're a little embarrassing. They're very formfitting," Dia objected.

"You have nothing to be shy of, Dia. Your body is lovely and attractive, like a fairy," Tarte reassured.

That wasn't flattery. Dia's chest was flat, and she wasn't very tall, but she didn't look like a child. Her frame was that of a slim model, and her waist was enviable.

"Oh, it's not like I don't have confidence in my appearance. I just feel shy about being ogled."

"There's nothing to be done about that. You have to do what it takes to ensure ease of movement," I declared.

The best way to ensure mobility was to wear formfitting attire. An inevitable consequence was that such garb displayed the contours of your form.

"Um, my lord, can I have a little time later for a personal errand? There's something I want to buy," Tarte suddenly asked.

"Sure, but what are you looking for?" I inquired.

"I—I need some new underwear. I've gotten bigger, and it's difficult to find that sort of thing in Tuatha Dé. The quality of such products is better in Milteu, too…"

Ah. So she's getting bigger.

For a moment, I thought I saw a coldness in Dia's eyes as she gazed at the fidgeting Tarte.

Our final stop for the day was at a blacksmith to buy some swords. My magic could forge blades, ones that were undoubtedly better than could be found in any store in Milteu, but I couldn't use them in public. For that reason, we'd sought out the most skilled crafter in the city.

No sooner had we entered than I felt someone watching me. It almost felt like we were being appraised.

"This isn't a toy store for kids. Get out of— Hmm? You don't look like ordinary children, especially you, boy. That blond girl, too. All right. I suppose you can pick something out." The man tending the store looked to be in his midthirties. He gave us a stern look when we first entered, but his expression quickly softened.

I'd heard he was picky about customers, but I hadn't known he took it to such an extreme.

"Thank you. Can we also purchase a sword for Dia…for this girl, please? I'm going to be training her."

"I don't mind. She seems quite capable. If you're gonna be teaching her, then she's no doubt worthy of using a sword of mine."

…I can't tell him, can I? We were only going to be using the blades we bought from him during classes. In any real combat scenario, we would be using far superior weapons. If he knew that, he'd probably turn us away.

"Thank you. We'll take a look around," I said. Then I began to inspect the different swords he had on display.

When choosing a blade, finding one that matched your physique and arm length was paramount. I picked out several weapons that seemed suitable and carefully examined their make. Then I decided on everyone's swords and had Dia and Tarte take a few test swings with the ones I'd chosen for them.

"It feels so nice!"

"Mine fits me well, too."

"…Hmm, actually, the grip isn't quite right. It would be better if you could change the material to something softer. Can we go ahead and get these?" I asked the blacksmith.

"I was about to propose the same thing. It makes me happy that you understand swords so well." While humming to himself, the craftsman unraveled the grip on the hilt and carefully and nimbly wrapped it with a softer material.

"There you are. The price will be…"

The total per weapon was roughly twice that of a typical blade, though that seemed appropriate. Not wanting to haggle, I paid the man.

"Thank you. These are high-quality products," I remarked.

"It's my pleasure. Customers like you are a rare blessing. Come back any time. Anyone who understands swordsmanship as well as you do is always welcome."

I thought I knew everything there was to know about Milteu. After encountering the food stall from earlier and this exceptional blacksmith, it became apparent that there were still many interesting places and people left to discover in Milteu.

After we finished making small talk with the owner, we walked outside.

I then noticed a group of three young men walking toward us. One of them was clearly wealthy.

I knew this because everything about him seemed to be screaming, *"I am an important person."* His two followers were undoubtedly guardsmen.

The rich man loudly instructed the others to go buy him a fitting sword. Perhaps he was preparing to go to the same academy Dia, Tarte, and I were.

Young nobles born with silver spoons in their mouths, much like that guy, were always the type to cause trouble.

After catching sight of Dia and Tarte, his eyes lit up, and his breathing intensified. His excitement was even visibly manifesting in his crotch.

Anyone could've guessed what was likely to happen next. Even if I told that upstart who I was, he looked the type to merely scoff at my lowly baron rank and try to whisk Dia and Tarte away.

Using my position as an assassin to scare the haughty noble was obviously not an option. This guy looked too stupid to understand the importance of the connections I held as a doctor, either.

Our social standing differences meant I couldn't win in an argument, and striking the young man would only lead to problems down the road.

What should I do here?

The answer was simple. All I had to do was nip the situation in the bud before he had a chance to cause any trouble.

I quickened my pace and walked ahead of Tarte and Dia.

Taking long strides, I passed one step ahead of the rich man as he advanced toward the girls. A few paces after we parted, he and his swollen crotch fell to the ground.

The guards' faces turned pale, and they ran to help him up.

I'd fired a Wind Bullet at the noble's chin, throwing off his coordination and causing him to fall.

Using a trick of mine, I hid my mana until the moment I cast the spell and knocked him out from his blind spot. Doing something like that after he'd tried to grab Dia and Tarte would've given him a reason to suspect me. Because I'd knocked him out before he made a move, however, there was nothing that could tie me to the fall.

My work complete, I slowed down and reunited with Dia and Tarte.

"That guy fell really suddenly. What happened to him?" asked Tarte.

"It's been scorching out lately. Maybe he got heatstroke?" conjectured Dia.

There was no need to tell them I'd just saved them from danger. That would only ruin the fun we were having.

"That's everything we needed to buy. What are we doing next?" Dia inquired.

"I made a reservation at an inn for us. Take the rest of the day to rest, then go sightseeing with Tarte tomorrow morning. I have something I need to do, so I won't be joining you," I replied.

"That's strangely vague. Are you hiding something, Lugh? Ah, are you meeting a local wife or something?"

"…No, nothing like that. It's for work."

Dia wasn't entirely wrong. I was visiting Maha, after all. Getting together with her wasn't without essential purpose, though.

"Hmmm. All right. Tarte, let's have fun together tomorrow."
Dia seemed to accept my explanation.

"Yeah, I know a lot of great shops I think you'll love," Tarte
answered cheerily.

"Great, I'm looking forward to it!"

It was nice to see Dia and Tarte warming up to each other.

I'd arranged a meeting with Maha because she'd recently
informed me that she'd finally obtained a divine treasure.

While I was genuinely happy she'd managed to find a powerful weapon, I was more interested in anything that could be
gleaned from studying a divine treasure. If I analyzed it, there was
a possibility I'd be able to make them myself.

The tavern room I'd reserved was one I'd learned about while I was working at the Balor Company. It was one of the most expensive places in Milteu, and people said there was no better place to stay in the city. Thankfully, the establishment's delicious food and scrupulous service justified the high price.

I spared no expense when it came to treating Dia and Tarte.

After dinner, the three of us retired to our room. The interior design was impressive. The place looked thoroughly cleaned, and the beds appeared comfortable and immaculate.

"That dinner was amazing! I wasn't familiar with the alcohol, but I was excited by how much there was. I thought I was used to eating fancy food, but there were so many dishes I'd never sampled before. It was so much fun!" Dia proclaimed.

"That's because Milteu is a harbor city. Delicacies from all over the world end up here. Milteu doesn't have very many local specialties, but tasting things from all over the world is part of this city's charm," I replied.

"Wow, now I really can't wait to go exploring tomorrow."

"You're right to be excited. It's impossible to be bored in this city as a tourist."

We sank into a lively discussion about Dia's sightseeing plans for the following day. Tarte would've typically participated in such a conversation, but something seemed to be making her uncomfortable.

"…My lord, is it okay for me to be treated to such fine things? I'm only your retainer. It doesn't feel right to me. I'm not used to being looked after. It makes me feel uneasy."

At the moment, Tarte wasn't wearing her servant clothes but was instead dressed in finer attire. I'd bought them for her before we arrived at the inn. Her Tuatha Dé servant clothes were cute, but I wanted to see her in something nicer every once in a while. That's why I'd picked out something I thought would look good on her. I'd done the same for Dia, too.

Tarte was lovely, and my chosen garments rendered her indistinguishable from a noblewoman. She'd turned the heads of many men while we were out in the city.

"You have to spread your wings now and then, Tarte. You've got to feel constricted doing servant work every day," I said.

"There's no way I'd grow weary of taking care of you, my lord!"

"I'm happy to hear you say that, but you need time for yourself… Also, I don't get many opportunities to eat with you. Eating with you makes dinner a lot more fun."

"You enjoy eating with me… That makes me happy. O-okay, I'll give in just for today."

Tarte always gave her all at her job, and it'd started to worry me. I needed to force her to rest once in a while.

"I get so jealous when I look at the two of you. You seem so natural together," admitted Dia.

"U-um, we've just known each other for a long time," Tarte said, blushing. She never handled that kind of teasing well. She

was so embarrassed, she hadn't even noticed that the candies she'd
been eating during our conversation had been dirtying her mouth.
How would she react if I wiped off her mouth right now? Feeling a
little mischievous, I picked up a napkin.

After reminding Dia and Tarte again that I had important matters
to attend to, I left the next morning.

I dyed my hair black, put on glasses, and used cosmetics to
disguise my face slightly. In only a short while, I had transformed
from Lugh Tuatha Dé into Illig Balor, a distinguished son of the
Balor family.

I was headed to the main store of the Balor Company cosmetics brand, Natural You. The storefront was on the first floor, while
the second floor was used for office space and storage.

I entered from the back, greeted the guards, and went inside.
I then climbed up the stairs and knocked on the door of Maha's
office.

"Enter."

"Hello, Maha."

"Welcome back, dear brother. It's been so long. I've been so
looking forward to this day."

Maha greeted me with a smile. She was an orphan whom I'd
adopted and raised. She'd proven herself very talented and oper-
ated the Natural You brand while Illig was away.

She had straight, glossy blue hair and was wearing a thin
layer of makeup. Her work attire—complete with full-length
pants—gave her a very enticing, intellectual sort of appeal. Like

Tarte and myself, she was fourteen years old. I would be remiss not to mention how beautiful she was, too.

"You're as pretty as ever, Maha."

"Why, thank you, dear brother. Don't you want to make this pretty woman yours? You can do what you like with me whenever you please, you know."

"I'll think it over," I answered, laughing awkwardly and sitting down on a sofa in the middle of the room. Unlike Tarte, Maha always said that kind of stuff directly.

She brewed some tea and sat down beside me. It smelled different from any tea I'd had before. Curious, I took a sip.

"This is an interesting tea leaf," I remarked.

"They were brought in from the south on a newly opened sea route. Their tea has a nice balance of sweet and bitter. It makes for a very relaxing drink. If you like it, I can send some to Tuatha Dé."

"That would be nice. There have been several things stressing me out lately, even at home. I would appreciate it if you could send them to me raw instead of boiled. I feel like I can figure out a way to improve on this tea, depending on how I prepare it."

"That's no problem. Let me know if you come up with a suitable preparation method. I want to expand our offerings beyond cosmetics soon."

Imported tea leaves were a valuable product. Enjoying them myself was all well and good, but they could also be used to entertain guests.

Maha and I enjoyed the tea and made idle conversation as she brought me up to date on recent events.

"So can I go ahead and see that thing you obtained for me?"

"Well, aren't you impatient? I was hoping we could chat for a bit longer. All right. I'll go fetch it for you."

Maha went to retrieve the item in question from a safe. It was wrapped up in old cloth, but I could feel mana emanating from it. Maha unraveled the fabric to reveal a small red and blue leather bag.

"This is a divine treasure?" I asked, dubious.

"Yes, it's called the Leather Crane Bag. Its unremarkable appearance made it a rather easy purchase," Maha answered.

Not all divine treasures were weapons. Many of them were tools. That appeared to be the case for this satchel.

"The way you explained it made it sound incredible. It doesn't seem all that useful," I observed.

"You'll change our mind once you see how it works."

Maha began to put all of the tea utensils into the bag. First, she stowed the teapot, then the tea leaf container, the cups, a basket full of sweets, and the milk pitcher. As if all that wasn't enough, she deposited a thick bundle of files, and finally a chair.

"This is a magic bag with an infinite capacity, so long as you supply it with mana. The weight never changes, no matter how many items are kept inside. It's so useful that any traveling trader would probably consider it a hugely unfair advantage."

"There isn't a merchant in the world who wouldn't want this, no matter the price," I remarked.

"...Considering its main function, yes. But it has a fatal flaw. Think about this logically, dear brother. If this bag were as good as it sounds, do you think I would have been able to purchase it for a price that didn't bankrupt Natural You?"

I shook my head. As the proxy representative for the Natural You brand, Maha had vast sums of money at her disposal. However, even with a veritable fortune, I doubted it would've been enough to buy such an incredible bag.

"Probably not. Balor, for example, would offer three times as much as us. He would be confident he could recover his costs in just two years. There is no way we could outbid the Balor Company," I said.

"That's exactly right. There is a fatal flaw that prevents this bag from being worth that much: Its capacity does not increase unless you supply it with a decent amount of mana, and as soon as the mana supply runs out, this happens."

Suddenly, all the contents of the bag exploded out at once.

"...I see. So you can't use it unless you're a mage, and even then, filling it with a constant stream of mana without pause would be draining. Can I take a look at it?" I requested.

"Go ahead," Maha replied.

I poured mana into the Leather Crane Bag. By doing so, I was able to get a sense of how much its capacity could be increased. If an average mage poured their full mana output into the satchel, the total would probably be enough to fit one horse-drawn carriage. However, any typical magic user wouldn't be able to hold that output for more than three minutes. The legendary item would, at best, be a glorified backpack. A normal rucksack that didn't drain mana was preferable.

"Now I see why merchants don't want it," I said.

"It's too unreliable for business. But you, dear brother...you can probably employ it as an assassination tool."

"You're right. I'm sure it'll come in handy."

As an assassin, being able to carry your weapons without drawing any suspicion was very important. That said, it felt like a waste to use a divine treasure for something so mundane.

As my mana capacity was one thousand times higher than the average mage's, using the bag continuously wasn't a problem. That everything would burst from the little container if my mana flow was interrupted for even a second was a big risk, though.

Actually, wait a second.

"I can probably make use of those," I muttered.

I took a Fahr Stone out of a small pouch. Fahr Stones were gems I carried around as weapons. I'd filled each one with as much mana as what three hundred normal mages could produce. I used them as explosives, but I'd also devised a way for the little spheres to release their mana at a steady rate.

I poured power into the Fahr Stone, made it so that it would continuously release magic energy, and put it into the Leather Crane Bag.

"If I do this, it won't put any strain on me, and the bag will have a steady supply of mana."

As I'd expected, the Leather Crane Bag absorbed the mana that the Fahr Stone was steadily releasing, and its capacity increased.

"How much do you think the bag can fit?" Maha inquired.

"Half a carriage's worth. I could increase the capacity even more if I hadn't set the Fahr Stone to release energy at such a slow rate," I answered.

"That's incredible. How would you feel about offering it and some Fahr Stones to the Natural You brand?"

"That would probably increase our profits, but I'm going to have to decline. I want to investigate this divine treasure thoroughly. If I can find some commonality between divine treasures, I might be able to develop a countermeasure for any I may have to deal with in the future. I might even be able to devise a way to create some divine treasures for myself. This bag is quite convenient. I'll make good use of it."

Such a wondrous pouch was more than a convenient tool. I

was already pondering ways to weaponize it. With a little bit of work, I believed it had the potential to become one of my trump cards against the hero.

"Thank you, Maha. You've found something truly extraordinary," I stated.

"Are words of thanks all you have for me?" Maha pressed.

"What, is there something else you want?"

"Yes. I want you to kiss me."

Maha leaned her face toward mine, glancing up at me amorously. No doubt she was just trying to tease me as she so often did.

"Ha-ha, if you don't want to, then we can just have lunch or something..."

"Okay, sure."

"Wait. What? You— WHAAAAA...?"

Maha, having fully expected me to turn her down, was shocked. I brought her close...and kissed her on the cheek. She blushed deep red and stiffened. There was no sign of her usual relaxed demeanor.

"How was that?" I asked.

Maha had trouble responding.

"...I...I don't..."

She looked down at her hands and finally managed to force out some words.

"...I-I'm so happy, and embarrassed, I don't think I'll be able to focus on work at all today."

She looked so cute that without thinking, I kissed her on the cheek again. Maha let out a panicked cry and froze up completely. Seeing her in such a state proved amusing, so I watched until she regained her composure.

Maha was always teasing me. There was nothing wrong with giving her a taste of her own medicine once in a while.

Likely because of the kiss, Maha pouted all through our lunch date. Even so, she couldn't wholly conceal her elation. Spending time with her like that was great fun.

One month had passed since that shopping trip to Milteu. Dia, Tarte, and I had finally arrived at the academy...or rather, the town surrounding the academy.

The academy was a two-hour carriage ride north of the royal capital. Apart from being a school, the place also functioned as a stronghold. It safeguarded the capital from any invaders coming south. Nowhere else in the world could you find so many mages in one place. Even students could be called upon to fight.

Concealed within the most massive bulwark in the country rested a modest-sized town.

My two companions and I were headed for the academy located in the middle of that settlement.

"We're here, my lord. It's almost time to put all of our studying to the test!" Tarte exclaimed.

"I'm exhausted from all the studying we've done this past month. It's gotten so bad that I've even had dreams about Alvanian history," Dia groaned.

The three of us had been spending the recent weeks preparing for our entrance exam.

The test didn't determine admission to the school, but rather, what class you were placed in. No noble's education was exactly the same. All students were divided into groups based on their level of knowledge to ensure efficient instruction. We'd been studying hard to be assigned to Class S, the best of all. I had a particular reason I needed to be placed high.

After passing the time by chatting, we arrived at the Royal Academy at last.

We told reception we were there to take the entrance exam, after which we were guided to an entrance that doubled as a plaza.

"Wow, there are so many people here," Tarte remarked with wonder.

"There are more adults here than there are students, though," observed Dia.

"Most of them are likely parents who've come to see their children off. I imagine they're worried about how their kids will do. The test score has a large impact on your family's worth," I explained.

"Wow, really? That's a little sad... Wait, what's that?!"

I followed Dia's line of sight and spotted an outrageously dressed individual.

"Didn't expect to see Prince Charming here at the academy," I quipped.

"Wha—? Surely that's overdoing it," Tarte added.

"That is a little much," Dia agreed.

Ahead of us was a boy riding a white horse. Perhaps in an attempt to match his steed, the young man was garbed in fancy alabaster clothing embroidered with gold thread. Everything about him was showy.

It did, however, look like he had the mana to back up that ostentatious attitude. He was quite handsome, and he wore his outfit well.

Quite unlike myself, he was flaunting his mana for all the

world to see. The emblem on his mount's bridle made it clear that he was the heir of House Gephis. He was one of the people Dad had told me to look out for at the academy. Not only did his family hold a dukedom, but it also possessed a spot in line for the royal throne.

The flamboyant young man winked as he passed by us. I initially thought it was directed toward Tarte and Dia, as those kinds of advances so often were. After a moment, I realized it had definitely been meant for me.

"What in the world is the heir of House Gephis thinking?" I muttered.

I hardly had any time to ponder the question, however, as an even greater commotion began to attract new onlookers. There was only one person who could cause a bigger stir than the son of a duke.

It's the hero.

He didn't introduce himself to anyone, but his overwhelming mana alone betrayed his identity.

It was such an intense amount of mana that you didn't even need Tuatha Dé eyes to perceive it.

The hero was surprisingly short. It was actually difficult to tell whether he was a boy or not. He looked utterly flustered. I wouldn't have been surprised if he broke down crying.

He bore absolutely no resemblance to Setanta, the man I'd fought when I'd saved Dia. For some reason, however, this timid kid gave off a similar aura.

People swarmed the poor boy, hoping to curry favor with the hero. I watched the scene from a distance. I also had plans for getting close to the hero, but it was too early to make my move.

If this teary-eyed young man really was the hero, then he'd

surely be placed in Class S. That's why Dia, Tarte, and I had studied so hard for the entrance exam. Being in the same division would afford many opportunities to approach the hero.

Out of the nearly one hundred mages in attendance, only eight were going to make it into Class S. Winning out over all the nobles was not going to be easy. To make things more complicated, I couldn't use House Tuatha Dé's special assassination techniques or any of the original magic I had created.

"It'll be hard...but not impossible."

I'd gained plenty of knowledge and experience during both my lives. Even without using my unique strengths, Dia, Tarte, and I should've been capable enough to accomplish anything the academy threw at us.

When it came time for the test to begin, students filed through the school entrance. A chorus of encouraging cheers echoed at our backs.

Things hadn't even commenced yet, and there was already such a huge ruckus. The posting of the exam results was liable to be pure pandemonium.

We followed a professor to the testing site, passing through many spacious hallways along the way.

First came the written portion.

"I'm so nervous. I know I'm going to end up in the same class as you, regardless of my grade, but as your retainer, I can't afford to embarrass you with a bad score."

Servant students took the test the same as everyone else, but they were always placed with their masters. They also didn't count toward the number of people in any given class. This was because a servant's primary purpose for coming to the academy was to support their master.

"You'll be fine. If you've memorized the stuff I've taught you in preparation for this exam, you'll do just fine. Or do you not trust me?" I inquired.

"Of course I trust you! I can do it!"

That honest simplicity was one of Tarte's best traits.

The instructor arrived punctually to announce the end of our break.

"Greetings, young fledglings who will soon bear the weight of the Alvanian Kingdom on your shoulders. Welcome to the Royal Knights Academy. First, you will take a written assessment, and then, after a one-hour break, you will take a practical evaluation. There are a couple of things you should be aware of before we start. I will take no questions, and leaving your seat is prohibited. If you leave your chair, your answers will be collected. That is all. I will now distribute the test booklet."

Packets of paper were placed facedown on everyone's desks.

"You may begin!"

No sooner had the proctor said those words than I flipped my test over and quickly scanned its contents.

The questions were largely what I'd expected. I hadn't spent the last month studying blindly. I'd used Illig Balor's information network to look into recent trends for the exam, and I'd shared what I'd learned with Dia and Tarte.

The first section was about Alvanian history and law. I was relieved to see that much of the material was composed of things I'd taught to the girls.

I had to laugh a little to myself at some of the problems. This assessment had clearly been written with a strong bias. Most of it was made up of history and laws the country wanted its nobles to be aware of. You could say it was exactly the sort of thing you'd expect from an academy that aimed to bring its aristocracy together for a common cause.

The next portion consisted of problems that tested cognitive ability and mathematics. I had no doubts that Dia and Tarte could handle that section.

The way things were progressing, I didn't suspect any of us would have trouble placing among the top scores. Sure enough, Dia and Tarte, who were sitting next to me, were flying through the test, their pencils racing.

As far as I could tell, only about 30 percent of the room was doing well.

Young nobles should've had no problem answering questions about their native history and laws, but that wasn't the case for lower-ranking aristocrats. Their parents typically taught them a version of the past that painted their lineage in a favorable light. They were only instructed on the parts of history their parents wanted them to know.

Even if a young person in such a position possessed a genuine interest in the past, books were expensive, and it was challenging to figure out which tomes contained true historical accounts and which had been modified. Many volumes were filled with complete nonsense.

On this assessment, the environment in which you were raised was even more important than your intelligence. Once again, I felt grateful to have been born a member of House Tuatha Dé.

Doing well on the written portion ensured that I'd be able to get away with holding back during the practical exam. I had to make sure I got high marks.

The first half of the test ended, and our break time began. It had ended up taking three hours, so we were all understandably exhausted. None of it had been broken up by subject, so we'd had to do the entire thing in one go.

One applicant had been fighting the urge to go to the bathroom the whole time. Eventually, they gave in and had to leave their seat, flushed and crying. An even more incredible student peed their pants intentionally so they could continue to take the test. Clearly, they didn't want to sully the reputation of their family name by leaving the exam for something trivial.

We all staggered outside like weakened zombies.

Dia, Tarte, and I walked into a spacious courtyard and found a bench to rest on.

Dia immediately set to talking excitedly about her performance on the test. "I'm sure I got over ninety percent right. That's a good score, but I'm nervous about how that will compare to everyone else."

"I don't think I did quite as well as that," Tarte admitted. "It was entirely stuff you taught us, though, my lord, so it was pretty easy for me, too!"

"I'm glad it went well. High marks should put you in the top ten," I praised.

"I can't wait for the results. How did you do, Lugh?" Dia inquired.

"Unless the teaching materials I used or the problems themselves were wrong, I got a perfect score," I stated.

"I'm not surprised. You're so smart, Lugh," praised Dia.

"We'll have to celebrate if you get the top grade! I'll treat us by making some delicious food!" Tarte declared.

"There's no need for that. There'll probably be something happening at the dorm to commemorate the new students entering the school," I responded.

"Aww, that's disappointing. I'll make some great dessert anyway!"

I forced a smile. Tarte was always putting me before herself.

Producing a basket, Tarte said, "A tired brain needs sweets! I got up early this morning to make these snacks."

"You must have been feeling really confident about the test if you felt you could get up early to make these. I thought you'd be the type to keep studying right up until the last second," Dia remarked.

"I just wanted to make both of you happy, Lord Lugh and Lady Dia," Tarte answered.

"I appreciate it. These look exceptional," I said.

The basket was full of steamed yellow buns. In Milteu, it was becoming a trend to steam bread instead of baking it. This gave the stuff a soft and spongy texture. A fair amount of egg yolk was then added to the bread to provide a rich flavor.

"All right, let's eat."

I tore off a piece of the squishy bread and put it in my mouth. A sweet, eggy sort of taste spread across my tongue. It was exactly the sort of thing I needed to relax and recharge my brain.

"Tarte, this is delicious," I praised.

"Yeah, it really is. You should make more of these sometime," added Dia.

"I'd be happy to! These did turn out quite good."

Tarte's steamed sweets were a kind that neither my mom nor I had ever made before.

When did Tarte start finding recipes on her own? I wondered. It was good to see her gain more confidence.

Dia prepared some tea as thanks for Tarte. She didn't have any tea utensils, but she created some using earth and fire magic.

In the middle of our intense entrance exam with the dignity of every royal house riding on it, the three of us enjoyed a laid-back respite, eating buns and sipping tea. It wasn't long, however, before someone arrived to ruin our peaceful moment.

"Hey, it's the Tuatha Dé family. Would you mind if I joined this tea party?"

A handsome boy with bright blond hair was approaching.

I didn't want anyone to ruin our precious break time, but this boy belonged to one of the four major dukedoms.

"Not at all," I replied.

"Thank you. I'm sure you know my name already, but allow me to introduce myself anyway. I am Naoise Gephis."

"My name is Lugh Tuatha Dé. It is a pleasure to meet you."

"Ha-ha-ha, come now, you don't need to be so polite. At this academy, strength is everything. That's what the royal family says. And don't you think that we, who have sworn our unfailing allegiance to the king, should comply with the word of the crown?"

That's not something I would've expected someone from a duke's family to say.

"All right, I'll speak freely," I agreed.

"Please do. I feel much more at ease that way. Hey, would you mind if I tried one of those treats you've got there?" Naoise asked, turning toward Tarte.

"N-no, not at all. But I'm sure they fall short of the sort of sweets a noble of your standing is used to tasting...," Tarte answered shyly.

Heedless of Tarte's warning, Naoise grabbed a steamed egg bun and ate it.

"That's delicious. It has a simple appeal that the confections of my castle lack. I like it. I think I'll have another."

He wasn't acting at all like an aristocrat. However, Naoise cut such an elegant figure that he could do anything, and it'd look as beautiful as a painting.

"What do you want? I imagine you have a purpose beyond eating," I pressed.

"I just wanted to meet you. I was hoping you'd consider joining me and helping me to achieve my dream. Before my graduation, I want to gather the very best the academy has to offer so that we can achieve great things together. Most especially, I want you, Lugh Tuatha Dé. That's why I approached you first," Naoise replied.

...How much does he know?

I hadn't demonstrated my real strength yet, and there was no way Naoise wanted to talk to a simple baron's son. Many people at the academy hailed from much more distinguished lineages. I would've understood if he knew of my covert profession, but the only ones privy to that secret were the royal family and a certain dukedom.

"Why me?" I questioned.

"Because you're more skilled than anyone here," Naoise returned.

"Surely the hero dwarfs me."

"The hero is strongest in terms of brute strength, and that certainly has its uses, but you are more impressive overall. But we can leave things at a greeting for today. Think it over for me… Let's change this rotten country together. You, of all people, should understand how necessary that is. If we don't act soon, it'll be too late. Those sweets were truly delicious, by the way. Take this as thanks."

Naoise tossed a handkerchief toward Tarte and walked away. Tarte spent a few seconds sitting there dumbfounded before she looked down at the cloth.

"Wow, this is really nice."

"It's made of the very best silk, and the gold thread embroidered into it is top rate, too. Selling this would net you enough money to live on for a year," I explained.

"I—I can't take this. I'm going to go give it back to him!" Tarte insisted.

"No, don't. He would actually see that as rude," I cautioned.

Tarte didn't know how to handle aristocratic gestures. She still clung to some of her old low-class habits.

"Hey, Lugh. What do you think he meant by changing this country?" Dia asked.

"…Any noble with a decent understanding of current affairs can see that Alvan is headed in the same direction as your Soigelian Kingdom. Naoise probably knows that. He might be trying to prevent ruination, or he may want to flip the country on its head if he believes it weak enough to suffer the same fate as Soigel. Either way, he seems quite ambitious," I remarked.

…The Royal Academy was a fitting place to gather personnel. You could approach people without the constraints of the nobility. It was a place unlike any other.

"I've never actually met anyone who's so openly stated that they want to change Alvan," Dia said.

"I can't tell if I should be impressed or think he's an idiot," I admitted.

When I first saw Naoise riding that white horse, I thought he was just some foolish dandy with overinflated self-esteem, but it turned out he had some fire in him. Perhaps he'd ridden that steed simply to leave a lasting impression.

A trumpet sounded. It wasn't signaling the end of the break, but rather the posting of our written test results. Dia, Tarte, and I headed toward the gathering crowd.

All right, time to see how we did.

All of the students crowded around a board where the written exam results were posted.

"Huh? Lord Lugh, they posted two pages for the written test results." Tarte cocked her head to one side.

"The servants' results are posted separately," I explained.

Because servants were placed in the same class as their masters and didn't count toward the class's registry, their scores were only recorded for reference. For that reason, their results were also posted on a different list.

"Yes, I did it! I ranked number one among the servants! I'm so relieved I didn't bring shame to Lord Lugh. 'Sixth' is written next to my name. What does that mean?"

"That means you did sixth best among all students. That's a rank to be proud of. You would be in a good position to make it into Class S even if you weren't a servant."

"That's really impressive, Tarte. Don't think I'm going to lose to you, though. Awww, I can't see the results at all through this crowd. I could just blast everyone out of the way with magic…"

The throngs of hopeful students were keeping us from our rankings. Dia was hopping up and down to see her results from the back, but her height gave her trouble.

"Don't get any dangerous ideas. Here, get on my shoulders."

"Wha—?"

I picked Dia up and sat her on my shoulders. As I did, she made a cute little squeal that was quite unusual for her.

"Thanks, but this is a little embarrassing... Also, I'm your older sister. Don't treat me like a child."

"Right now, you're my little sister, so it's okay. Can you see the results?"

"Yeah, I can see them. Let's see; you're number one, Lugh. Wait, no way, there are two people in first place. That pretentious boy from earlier is tied with you."

...I see, so Naoise isn't all talk.

"I'm number three. Aww, I'm disappointed. I really wanted to be number one."

"That's still an exceptional score, Dia. The practical portion tests magic and physical prowess. You'll get a very high score on the magic section, and your physical capabilities aren't bad, either. You're sure to make it to Class S."

"No one's going to beat me at magic. You're the one person I'd be slightly worried about," Dia admitted.

"No, you're better than me at magic," I replied.

Dia was so skilled that her incantations and her control of mana may as well have been art. I was superior when it came to simple mana output, but she had the advantage of subtle manipulation. Thanks to the goddess's intervention, I had the most excellent parameters an average human could possibly have, yet I still couldn't beat her. Dia was a spellcasting genius.

"Oh yeah, where did the hero place? You can probably see from up there," I asked.

"I don't know the hero's name, so I don't know," Dia answered.

"It's Epona. Epona Rhiannon."

After I'd heard the hero had appeared, I did some research. My efforts rewarded me with the knowledge that a hero wasn't born, but instead, awakened. He was a regular person, and then one day was suddenly reborn as the hero.

Epona Rhiannon was, like me, the child of a baron. Despite being a noble, he was born without mana, making him a disappointment. Baron Rhiannon had trouble producing another heir, so the house seemed to be in quite a bad situation. There were also several other things about Epona Rhiannon that were quite strange.

He was listed as male on his family register, but the more I looked into him, the more I wondered if he might actually be a girl. Seeing him in person did little to dissuade my doubts.

"Let's see... Epona, Epona... I can't find him at all. Ah, there he is. He's eighth from the bottom."

"...Thanks. That's all I wanted to know."

I set Dia back down.

Such a grade was typical of a normal baron's child. It hadn't been that long since he became the hero, and I'm sure he wasn't given the best education.

"I thought the hero would be an amazing person, but it doesn't look like he is," said Dia.

"I wonder what his life has been like. You can't get by on off-the-charts power alone," I responded.

That's exactly what the academy is for.

"Um, my lord. I feel like everyone's really been staring at us..."

"That's to be expected with the grades we got."

I'd become an object of attention for many girls from renowned noble families. There was nothing unusual about Naoise, the son of a duke, achieving the top rank, but it was strange for the lowly son of a baron to accomplish the same feat. Several people seemed vexed by it. Some clearly didn't care, however.

"I thought I was going to run away with this, but to think I might have an equal... You're just as brilliant as I thought you would be." I felt an overfamiliar pair of hands on my shoulders and turned around to see Naoise and his beautiful blond hair.

"Let's both do our best in the second half," I said.

"Of course. My goal is to become head of the class, and I won't lose... I'm saying this just in case, but don't even think about letting me win just because I'm the son of a duke. Being head of the class would hold no meaning if it was handed to me," Naoise replied.

"Got it. I won't hold back."

That wasn't entirely a lie. I planned to limit my power to a level that was okay to show, but that was the extent of my self-imposed restraint.

The bell announcing the end of our break rang, and the professor returned and proclaimed the start of the second half of the test.

The practical exam was now halfway over. The first half had been a test of our magic abilities.

To begin, we declared our strongest element, and then we were graded on our ability to chant and perform three predetermined spells.

We were graded on our mana output volume, amount of mana maintained during elemental conversion, incantation speed, and our spells' accuracy.

I performed my incantations while repressing my power down to the high end of what a typical mage would've been capable of. I ended up placing second.

"Hmm-hmm, as I said, no one can beat me when it comes to magic," said the self-satisfied girl who placed first.

"I knew you would top the chart, Lady Dia! The beauty of your incantations entranced me," Tarte praised.

"No matter how many times I see you do it, I still don't understand how you pull off elemental conversion while losing so little mana," I said.

Mana had to be converted into magic. Conversion was an essential skill, and despite the aggravating amount of time I'd spent trying to get better at it, I just couldn't surpass Dia.

The standard mana retention for a typical mage was about 60 to 70 percent, but I could get to a little under 90. Dia, however, always achieved 95 percent.

This wasn't only important for keeping your mana consumption rate low and increasing your spells' force. Unconverted mana hampered your casting, so a skilled elemental conversion also increased your accuracy.

There was only about a 5 percent difference between my elemental conversion and Dia's, but that 5 percent made a big difference.

"I only placed sixth... Lord Lugh has taught me so much. I should have done better," Tarte bemoaned, her shoulders drooping.

Tarte achieved such a good grade because I'd been teaching her. More specifically, I'd been using my Tuatha Dé eyes to observe her mana and identify points where she needed to improve. Because I could see mana, something a regular person could only feel, I was able to instruct and give corrections at an extremely efficient rate. The combination of Tarte's hard work and my special training had allowed her to become as skilled as she was.

"You did well. The only people ranked above you are veritable monsters when it comes to mana."

The people who placed above Tarte were me, Dia, Naoise, the hero Epona, and the prodigy of a family known for specializing in magic.

Watching Naoise's incantations confirmed how hard of a worker he was. He possessed a keen sense for magic, and there was no doubt he had an elite teacher. But he couldn't have achieved all he had without blood, sweat, and tears.

On the other hand, it was preposterous that Epona ended up ranking as high as he did. His elemental conversion was terrible. He only retained 50 percent of his mana at best, which was lower than average. His incantations were also slow, and his accuracy was lacking. However, his mana output was absurdly high, and with that alone, his overall grade passed Tarte's.

Dia and I both watched his test in astonishment.

"Dia, I can't believe what I just saw. How did a basic spell like Fireball end up turning into that?"

"Yeah, I don't want to believe it, either. He achieved that level of force despite how clumsy and unskilled his casting was. What would have happened if his incantation was decent?"

As the name suggested, Fireball was a spell that produced a fist-sized ball of flame. The ball drifted softly through the air and was hot enough to burn skin.

That didn't quite describe the hero's Fireball, though.

The hero's spell was so scorching hot that it looked like a

compressed sun. It instantly surpassed the speed of sound and turned everything in its path to ash before disappearing off into the distance. It ended up blasting a hole through the bulwark that served to repel invasions. It was a miracle there were no casualties.

...*This is what he is capable of with a beginner's spell. He probably doesn't just have ridiculously high mana capacity, but also a skill that strengthens spells.*

Just the thought of fighting him made me shudder.

At the moment, his slow incantations and poor accuracy made his spells unusable in battle. If the academy's teachings brought him to even an average skill level, he could quickly become too much for me to handle.

Next, the physical test began. Proctors tested us on various measurements, including physical strength, leaping ability, stamina, reaction time, and more.

Tarte shone on this part of the assessment.

At first glance, this portion appeared to be a simple competition of physical strength, but it was more than that in actuality. To a mage, the technique of increasing your body's physical capabilities was essential. Instead of using mana to enhance every part of your body, it was better to focus on portions that were connected to movement.

Not many people were capable of focusing their mana only on specific body parts, though. As far as I could tell, the only participants who could were me, Tarte, Naoise, and three others. Dia was still learning.

The hero, however, as if in mockery of that advanced skill,

displayed overwhelming ability and placed first in every category despite his clumsy talent with mana.

I didn't feel like I had any chance of beating him. It felt wrong even to compare myself to someone so exceptional. Calling him a monster didn't even begin to describe him.

Those who'd lost interest in the hero after his pitiful score on the written test immediately returned to praise him.

What caught my eye was how suffocated the hero seemed by all the attention. It looked like he didn't handle personal interaction very well... That hardly created any problems for me, though. For people who had an expert grasp of human nature, that kind of personality was easier to deal with.

Before long, the final part of our exam began. This last bit tested our combat skills.

Knights in active service from the Royal Alvanian Order served as the students' opponents. Their weapons were blunted, and there were doctors at the ready.

The majority of students weren't expected to have any chance of defeating a knight. More than victory, proctors were observing what sorts of actions students took during the sparring matches.

The arena at the Royal Academy was huge, with six rings set up within it. Tarte had to leave for the waiting room because her match was one of the first. This left Dia and me alone to watch from the stands.

A few matches had already ended.

"It looks like there are a lot of impressive people here," Dia observed.

"Yeah. I'm glad at this chance to see the strength of our class-mates so soon," I answered.

House Tuatha Dé wasn't the only family that valued combat education. Other clans were known for producing knights. They staked their statuses on military prowess and trained their off-spring in the ways of war from an early age. There were even some students who matched the active knights in skill.

"Lugh, do you think Tarte will be okay?" Dia asked.

"She'll be fine. You know how strong she is. Actually, now that I think about it, you haven't seen Tarte in a real fight yet, have you?"

"Hmm, I guess not. So she's that strong, huh? I need to watch closely."

Tarte used a spear and surpassed the strength of most active knights. I had trained her as a Tuatha Dé and instilled in her knowledge and techniques from my previous life.

Tarte entered the ring. She was already holding the spear that she usually concealed beneath her skirt.

She faced her sparring partner, but before the match began, the knight suddenly bowed. The action caused a stir to run through those in the stands. It was clearly not a customary courtesy bow. The knight appeared to be genuinely thankful for something.

Tarte looked bewildered and unsure of what to do. The knight then said something to her, and Tarte's face flushed deep red, after which she frantically made some kind of request. The arena grew noisy as people wondered what was going on.

Tarte and the knight immediately began the match as if noth-ing had happened, and Tarte ended up winning. She attracted everyone's attention; the shock that a female servant defeated a knight was palpable.

Many people were suggesting that Tarte had seduced the knight into throwing the match. They couldn't believe that someone who was both a girl and a servant could've won in a fair fight. Two students sitting next to us were among those spreading rumors.

"I have to get out of here for a bit. What these people are saying is too terrible," Dia said.

"Hey, don't worry about them. Anyone who can actually fight can easily tell Tarte's true skill from the way she handles her spear. The people who don't get it don't deserve your attention," I responded.

"That's true, but..."

"Relax. They'll get what's coming to them. More importantly, your turn is coming up."

If Dia let her emotions get the best of her now, it could affect her performance. Unlike her, I could use those feelings to enhance my capabilities. I'd said what I did to calm her down, but I was just as angry at all the people insulting Tarte. I promised to make them regret making such accusations.

"Ah, I have to go. Cheer me on...and take care of Tarte, okay?"

Dia left, and Tarte returned shortly afterward. I asked her what she and the knight had been talking about before the match.

"Um, he recognized me from when I was getting combat experience on the battlefield. He said I saved his life once, and he thanked me."

"...So you met back then, huh?"

While we were in Milteu, I'd decided that Tarte didn't have enough combat experience. Using some of my connections, I got her onto the battlefield for proper action.

"Yes. I would never have expected to see someone I fought with back then, so I was surprised."

"It looked like you made some request. What was that about?"

"Um, well, he said he was going to tell the professors about my service on the battlefield and the embarrassing nickname I was given during that time. He meant well, but I asked him not to do it."

"You do realize that now you have to tell me what your nickname was."

"You can't share this with anyone, my lord... It was the Electric War Maiden... I really don't want to be called that in front of anybody."

The Electric War Maiden. It fits her fighting style.

Tarte's physical strengthening was exceptional, and her mastery of wind allowed her to reach incredible speeds. Her flexibility and reflexes even afforded her full-body control at top speed.

The Electric War Maiden was quite a fitting moniker. Tarte did possess lightning-fast speed.

She wasn't without her weaknesses, though. Tarte was still growing, which could cause problems as she got even faster. At her current top speed, she could only barely maintain full-body control. Any swifter, and it would no doubt become difficult for her to execute her attacks.

If things continued as they were, her speed would surpass her ability to perceive objects in motion. She'd probably need Tuatha Dé eyes before long.

"Oh yeah, when is your fight, my lord? I've been looking forward to it so much!"

"I'm one of the last, so it's gonna be a little while. For now, it looks like Dia's match is beginning, so let's cheer her on."

"You should have told me that sooner!"

Dia's match commenced. She was wielding a sword. It was clear from the beginning that she was at a disadvantage. She put up a good fight, but the match ended in defeat after five minutes.

Dia's main fighting style was with magic. I'd started instructing her on the basics of close-quarters combat, but she was still a learner. She also got really unlucky with her opponent. He was very talented, even for a knight. He wasn't the sort of opponent Dia could best.

"Aw, she was so close."

"She did well enough to get a good score. What's important is she demonstrated her capabilities. At her current strength, we can't ask for more than that."

The crowd clapped for Dia. She had given it her best effort, after all.

Dia left the ring, and Epona took her place. His opponent was the commander of the Royal Order. The man was top among the knights not just in rank but also in strength. He was wearing a full suit of armor. It wasn't any ordinary plate, either. It was made of a scarce metal called mithril, which was significantly stronger than iron armor.

To some, it might've seemed excessive, but I thought it was a wise decision. Even with the commander's elite equipment, the risk of being killed in a match with the hero was high.

No sooner had the bout begun than the hero disappeared. Immediately, he reappeared in front of the commander with his little fist raised. The commander instantly vanished from sight. A moment later, there was an intense boom.

As I scanned the area, a second thundering sound echoed through the arena. I finally found the commander collapsed in the stands.

Peering at Epona, I saw broken fragments of mithril scattered around him.

...He smashed that armor with his fist.

The hero was terrifying. I'd thought I understood that already, but this was ridiculous.

Not even my Tuatha Dé eyes could register his movement. If it had been me standing there in place of the commander, I would've suffered the same fate. Unfortunately, Epona was only going to get stronger from here on out.

"Epona's not quite at Setanta's level yet, but he'll surpass him within a year. Actually, it might only be a month," I muttered.

I wasn't sure assassinating him would even be possible.

"I need to become stronger," I vowed to myself.

My turn was fast approaching, and I needed to head down to the ring.

"Tarte, I'm heading down."

"Okay, I'll cheer as loud as I can!"

My test results all but guaranteed my placement in Class S at this point. I'd planned on playing it safe by losing intentionally while making it look like I put up a good fight, but seeing the hero's absurd strength left me fired up.

I might just have to put in a little real effort.

My match was one of the last ones to be held.

Students were heavily invested in these final rounds. The reason for that was simple: The last two contestants had the highest two grades on the exam thus far. This final battle would determine who the head of the class was.

Dia did great on the magic test, but her standing had dropped after the physical examination. Tarte was the opposite. Epona's rank was bogged down by his poor performance on the written portion.

As a result, Naoise and I were the clear forerunners.

Naoise and I lined up next to each other and then turned toward our respective rings.

"Lugh, I said this earlier, but don't even think about giving me the top spot... I want to win fair and square, with my strength alone."

"I swear I'll give it my all."

Naoise was staring straight at me, as if looking right through to the other side. I risked him realizing I was holding back if I wasn't careful about how I restrained myself.

We went to our rings without saying another word. My opponent was already waiting for me.

I would never have thought we would both be facing vice-commanders of the Royal Order. This wasn't going to be an easy fight. It looked like the academy wanted to give its two best applicants a special sort of challenge.

"Lord Lugh, you can do it!"

"If you beat me, I'll make you a large serving of pancakes for breakfast tomorrow!"

Tarte and Dia were cheering for me from the stands. It was nice of them, but I couldn't help but feel a bit embarrassed.

"Well, aren't you popular? You're making me jealous," needled my opponent.

"My family can get a little overenthusiastic…," I responded.

"Don't worry about it. That's just extra motivation for me. I can't just let you use me to show off to those cute girls, little Mr. Popular."

He's projecting unbelievable malice.

The vice-commander had seemingly forgotten he was sparring with a student as part of an exam.

"That's rather childish of you," I observed.

"Ha-ha-ha. You're probably right. But I won't have to hold back against you."

It wasn't a surprise that the vice-commander recognized my ability. Once a person reached a certain level of mastery, they could gauge their opponent's skill from their breathing and the way they walked.

We both tightened our grip on our respective weapons.

I'd decided to go with a sword for this fight. In truth, I was better with knives, martial arts, and guns, but I wasn't all that bad with a sword. Long-bladed weapons were too clumsy for assassination. I hoped that would allow me to conceal my usual fighting style and avoid giving away any Tuatha Dé secrets.

…Also, if I fight with a knife, I may end up killing him on reflex.

The proctor asked if my opponent and I were ready, and I nodded.

"Begin!" came the announcement.

The vice-commander and I both immediately seized up, however. The reason we stopped was that we felt a tremendous amount of mana coming from the neighboring ring.

Naoise was the source. He'd aimed his sword at his opponent's eyes and used his full mana output to strengthen his body.

His physical strengthening technique was incredible. Not only was he powerful and elegant, but he was also overflowing with a combative spirit.

I could tell from the mana coming off him that he intended to fight his opponent head-on with his full strength, without resorting to any cheap tricks. It was inspiring.

...Man, this is out of character for me, but I'm getting really fired up. I was thinking about taking it slow at first and waiting for my opponent to make the first move, but screw that.

"HAAAAAAAAAHHHHH!"

It'd spoil the fun if I didn't put in some real effort. An assassin should never have done something so careless. At that moment, however, I wasn't an assassin; I was a swordsman.

I could see the vice-commander's mana capacity with my Tuatha Dé eyes. I adjusted my strength to match his exactly. It was a far cry from my full power, but I was still using much more mana than the average mage was capable of.

...Our mana capacity should be about the same now. That means the match will be decided by our sword skills, physical strengthening techniques, how well we read each other, and our mental fortitude.

The vice-commander grinned broadly. The one paired with Naoise did the same.

"The new students this year have some spark to them. I like it. I'm not going to hold back."

"Same here. This should be fun. But there's no way in hell I'm gonna lose. We have the pride of the Royal Order to uphold."

The vice-commanders both enveloped themselves with all the magic power they could muster.

All four of us were releasing a colossal amount of mana. Every spectator eagerly awaited what would come next.

I focused everything on the man standing before me.

I was an assassin through and through. That was true in my previous life and this one as well. I was trained in straightforward melee combat, but only as a backup if covert methods failed. Additionally, I also wasn't using any Tuatha Dé assassination techniques or surprise attacks of any kind.

Let's see what I'm capable of with orthodox swordsmanship.

The vice-commander and I swung our swords at the same time. He was slightly faster and had a little more weight behind his motion.

I made sure we were strengthening our physical capabilities with the same amount of mana. My strengthening technique was slightly better.

When it came to raw power, however, I was the clear loser. I'd used Rapid Recovery to train my body as efficiently as possible, but I was still only fourteen years old.

On top of that, the vice-commander was an experienced blade wielder, and his body was optimized for using one. That put me at a slight disadvantage.

I was sure to be defeated if our swings made even contact, so I lowered my sword a little and relaxed my muscles. Right before our blades impacted, I drew back and avoided the attack. It was the sort of move only someone with Tuatha Dé eyes could've made.

My evasion had been a success, but the vice-commander read the situation and immediately pursued me. While I avoided two more swings, it was clear my opponent had expected me to do so. He was trying to drive me into a difficult position, and the tactic was working.

I wouldn't be able to dodge the vice-commander's next attack. If I got hit, my posture would crumble, and I'd lose all ability to counterattack.

Continuing to fight in an orthodox manner meant my inevitable defeat in seven or eight moves. My suspicion that I wouldn't be able to win in a straightforward swordfight had been correct.

I had two choices.

The former choice was to continue as I was and lose while giving it my all in a fair duel. The latter option was to employ other fighting techniques. My repertoire was filled with maneuvers other than those exclusively used for assassination. I was worried they'd still seem too conspicuous, however.

Guess I'll just lose.

The moment I thought that, however, I heard Tarte and Dia cheering.

…That's right, those two are watching. I can't embarrass myself in front of them. I can't lose.

Rather than fixing my crumbling stance, I used my backward momentum to perform a spinning kick. From my position, my leg could reach farther than the vice-commander's sword. I caught him by surprise and successfully planted my foot in his stomach.

The kick was strengthened by mana and normally would've had enough power to kill.

"Tch..."

My kick had a lighter impact than I'd expected. My opponent avoided the full force of the blow by jumping back. His reaction time was incredibly quick.

I needed to pursue him. He created distance between us when he jumped backward, rendering me unable to reach him with a direct attack, so I threw my sword at him.

"...Hey, kid, that's not very knightly of you. But still, not bad."

He deflected the attack, and that's exactly what I wanted to happen.

I charged while the vice-commander's attention was still focused on my sword. Crouching to escape his field of vision, I slipped into a blind spot.

Now positioned behind the vice-commander, I leaped up at him. I didn't have my sword, so I swung at him using my scabbard. The point of the scabbard was made of metal. A direct blow to the temple should've knocked him unconscious.

"Not so fast!"

"Man, you're pretty good..."

My strike had been from my opponent's blind spot on his non-dominant side, but he was still able to block it with a gauntlet. That vice-commander title wasn't just for show.

He repelled a second thrust using his sword, and my scabbard flew from my hands, whirling through the air. It wasn't a surprising development. Scabbards were much more challenging to grip than proper weapons, so it wasn't hard to knock one aside.

"This ends here, kid." The vice-commander raised his sword overhead to prepare for a downward swing.

Without a weapon, I was at a considerable disadvantage. The best course of action was to get as close to the vice-commander as possible, so I rushed forward.

"What the—?"

He wouldn't be able to swing his sword down at me if I was at point-blank range. Hesitating to close the distance could've cost me the match.

What's more, I wasn't moving in just to avoid. I was preparing an attack of my own.

I rushed forward, spun in the air using my momentum, then used all my strength to hit him with a palm strike as I landed. Using this method, I could release a powerful attack even at point-blank range.

"Haaah!"

My motion landed with the sound of an explosion.

It wasn't a simple palm strike. The maneuver was an intricate move designed to create a massive burst of mana and energy within my opponent.

The vice-commander was sent flying through the air. He came to land outside the ring after spinning five full times. The proctor rushed over to him. And then...

"The winner is the first-year student, Lugh Tuatha Dé!" He called out my name as the victor.

"Phew, I pulled it off."

It ended up looking like a one-sided match, but I would've lost if I hadn't spent most of the match stalling. That vice-commander had actually blocked two attacks that were supposed to defeat him. It was only my third attack that'd done him in.

The reaction from the crowd was divided into three camps.

"Whoo-hoo! You're so amazing, Lord Lugh! You beat a vice-commander!"

"Hmm-hmm, I never doubted you. You're Lugh, after all. When you get back, I'll give you a kiss!"

People were cheering enthusiastically like Tarte and Dia. Some others were dumbfounded that a first-year defeated a vice-commander of the knights. The last group was filled with those who were annoyed that a lowly baron's son was enjoying such success.

A doctor rushed over to the fallen vice-commander and began treating him. After about a minute, the vice-commander opened his eyes.

He'd focused all of his mana and spirit into his stomach the moment my attack connected. I'd succeeded in knocking him unconscious, but I could tell when I struck him that I hadn't hurt him too badly.

"This is disappointing. All I ended up doing was making you look good, little Mr. Popular. You caught me off guard by using that rough style of combat instead of the nobility's elegant swordsmanship. If only I'd seen that coming, I might've won."

"I was planning to fight in a more standard style at first, but as soon as the match began, I realized it wasn't going to work. I ended up winning, but I feel like I lost."

We exchanged bitter smiles, then I reached out my hand and helped him up.

"Well, regardless, you beat me handily. I'm looking forward to what you'll achieve in the years to come. You should join the Royal Order when you graduate," the vice-commander offered.

"I'll think about it," I answered with a bow.

I'd ended up winning, but I knew that my method of victory had lost me a few points. The judges undoubtedly preferred

students who succeeded by overpowering their opponents with traditional methods.

Wondering how Naoise was doing, I looked over at the ring next to me. His intense battle was still raging. Unlike me, he was using proper swordsmanship.

Naoise was employing the royal style. It was Alvan's most prestigious bladework form and had been improved upon by countless instructors throughout the generations. It tended to lean too hard into the beauty of sword fighting, but it was powerful nonetheless.

Naoise was performing it to perfection. I don't think there were many as competent as him.

The battle seemed to be a stalemate, but Naoise was slowly gaining the advantage. His superior mana output was making the difference. The vice-commander was more skilled in terms of swordsmanship, but Naoise's magical power gave him a more significant edge.

When the vice-commander ran out of mana, the battle was as good as over.

The vice-commander lost his physical strengthening, which threw off his stance. Naoise saw through this immediately.

Recognizing the vice-commander's weak grip on his sword, Naoise delivered a decisive blow and knocked the weapon out of his opponent's hand. He then put his blade to his opponent's throat.

"I win."

"I surrender. Geez, the rookies this year are no joke. The commander and we vice-commanders were all defeated... Losing puts a bad taste in my mouth, but it looks like this country has a bright future ahead of it."

After Naoise's match ended, the crowd burst with applause.

Unlike when I won, everyone was cheering. His victory sparked no jealousy among the students, as there was nothing unusual about a duke's son winning.

It didn't bother me. I had Dia and Tarte's support, and that was good enough. When I won, they'd cheered for me louder than anyone else.

Naoise smiled at me. "I have no idea which of us is going to come out on top."

"It'll all come down to the judges," I said. In reality, though, Naoise had an 80–90 percent chance of being named head of the class. The professors preferred that kind of traditional fighting style. It would also be easier for people to accept the son of a duke as head of the class over a baron's child. There wasn't much of a difference between us on the assessment, so Naoise was sure to be chosen if they decided based on opinion.

After another break, the students once again gathered at the entrance of the academy.

The gate was opened, and parents all rushed through at once. They were eager to see where their kids ranked among the student body. Placement affected a noble house's prestige.

First, the rosters for all the classes except for Class S were posted. Shrieks and roars of anger sounded in response.

Some cried, some fainted, and some were even choked by their parents or told they were being disowned.

So much for the elegance of aristocracy.

Before long, the time came for the reveal of the top eight students.

A middle-aged man walked up onto a stage. He was the head-master of the academy.

"Greetings, everyone. It is now time to introduce the members of Class S. I will start with the servants: Beryl, Cranta, and Tarte. I want to give special attention to Tarte, who performed well enough to place in Class S even as a general student."

This was met with applause.

That officially confirms my spot in Class S. Turns out there weren't many mages among the servants. I guess that shouldn't have been too surprising.

"Now, on to the students. Ranking eighth was Belruk Crutalis."

Each student went up on stage after their name was announced, every one of them looking very proud of themselves. It meant a lot to make it into Class S.

The hero Epona was also called. He ended up in fourth. The written test had really held him back.

And then...

"These top three students are all excellent individuals who will surely serve as leaders for this new generation. Claudia Tuatha Dé, congratulations on placing third."

Dia was called. "See you up there," she said, and she ran up to the stage.

All eyes then fell to Naoise and me. We were the only ones whose names hadn't been announced. One of us was going to be proclaimed the head of the class.

The headmaster paused to clear his throat. He then opened his mouth slowly.

"Lugh Tuatha Dé..."

That meant I was second, inferior only to Naoise.

I knew that would happen, so I didn't feel down about it. Not being number one actually suited me better, as I would stand out less.

"...And Naoise Gephis. Both of you tied for first and will share the honor of being head of the class."

A grinning Naoise clapped me on the shoulder, and we headed for the stage together.

"I didn't think we would end up tied. It's a shame I couldn't beat you...but I'm delighted to see one of my men doing so well."

"I never said I was your man."

"Trust me; you will be. I've already decided it."

This guy is ridiculous.

Amid adulation and envy, Naoise and I made our way to the stage.

How in the world did Naoise get to like me so much?

It wasn't all bad, I supposed. His distinct presence was sure to keep attention away from me. With him around, fewer people would approach me unhappy that I was having such success despite being a baron's son.

Regardless of how things played out, I succeeded at making it into the same class as the hero. Now all I had to do was become his friend. That didn't seem a particularly daunting task.

Tying for first with Naoise had garnered me quite the reputation.

"The headmaster suddenly summoning us like this must mean he thinks rather highly of we four," Naoise remarked.

"Yeah, probably. He did single us out instead of calling all of Class S," I responded.

Our other classmates went straight to the classroom, but Naoise, Dia, and I—the students with the three highest grades—had been called to the headmaster's office. Tarte's presence had also been requested.

"Your little sister and your retainer are both very skilled, Lugh. When you come to serve me, you'll bring them along, too, right?" Naoise asked.

"Once again, I haven't said a word about helping you."

"Ha-ha-ha, relax. I'll make sure you change your mind," Naoise answered with a laugh. He was starting to trouble me. As the son of a duke, he wouldn't be incapable of forcing me to join up with him.

The only ones who could oppose a duke were the royal family and the archduke. If this became a serious problem, there was a duke with a strong connection to House Tuatha Dé who could help out. That duke's clan was the only house other than the royal family that knew of the secret profession of House Tuatha Dé.

"I know that face. You're thinking about your family, aren't you? Well, you have nothing to worry about. I'll take care of them," Naoise declared flippantly.

"Do you know what you're saying?" I asked.

"Of course. If I can't manage that much, how will I ever change this country? But we can discuss this later. We've arrived at the headmaster's office."

After giving the word to his own servant, Naoise knocked on the door.

"Enter," called out a deep voice. We opened the door and walked inside.

The headmaster was a middle-aged man with white hair. Despite that, he was a powerful-looking man. His physique didn't betray a single hint of weakness. His white hair looked like the mane of a lion, and he had a special kind of presence about him.

His strength was well-documented. He had been the Royal Order commander until his retirement five years ago and was said to be the strongest and best instructor in the organization's history. Even now, many thought him to be more capable than the current commander.

"Naoise, Lugh, Claudia, and Tarte. I am very thankful to the four of you for attending this school. Especially in a time such as this," the headmaster began.

"Are you talking about the hero, sir?" I asked.

"That is correct. Epona is powerful. But he is raw, and he needs people to support him. The four of you are more than fit to be his friends and companions. Before long, I will have the four of you tour the country at his side."

For a moment, Naoise looked like he was going to reject the headmaster's proposal outright, but he restrained himself.

"Headmaster, those are very kind words, but we, too, are still untrained. There are plenty of knights and mages more capable than us. Even if our skill is as great as you say, we lack true combat experience and will surely fail to deal with any unforeseen circumstances that may arise. We are not worthy of being the hero's companions. Please reconsider."

That was unexpected. As obsessed as Naoise was with success and the limelight, I didn't think he would refuse. Traveling with the hero was the greatest honor imaginable. If all went well, it was an opportunity to win the rare privilege of having helped to save the world.

"Cease this humility. On the entrance exam, you and Lugh proved you are already stronger than a vice-commander of the Royal Alvanian Order... There aren't many people who can boast that kind of strength," the headmaster stated.

"But as I said, we lack experience and will not be able to deal with unexpected circumstances," Naoise insisted.

"Then become stronger. That's what this academy is for."

"I cannot accept such a great responsibility."

"Hmph, you're still resisting? Quit this dog and pony show, Naoise Gephis. I guarantee you, being a companion of the hero will not be a detour for what you want to accomplish. Do you understand me?"

"...Very perceptive, Headmaster. Okay, I promise to devote my strength to the hero."

Naoise bowed in a manner befitting one of his stature. He probably realized it would be a waste to argue any more. This speed of ascertainment was one of his strengths.

I understood the situation, but there was one thing that was bothering me.

"Headmaster, why didn't you call the hero here? What do you have planned for us? If all you wanted was for us to be his companions, then it would have made more sense to have him here, too," I said.

"How astute, Lugh Tuatha Dé. You are strong, but your intelligence is even more impressive," praised the headmaster.

I had a feeling the older man wasn't only going by the exams when he said that. The headmaster's saying he wanted us to be the hero's companions meant he'd used every means at his disposal to look into our backgrounds. That being the case, this wasn't the time for me to play dumb.

"What I think you want from us is to be Epona Rhiannon's chains. You aren't telling us to follow him out of a sense of duty, but as friends. That's why it needs to be us. There are plenty of people more skilled, but only we can fulfill that sort of role. Honestly, though, I feel a little reluctant," I said.

"Hoh-hoh-hoh, you are correct. I would expect no less from a Tuatha Dé. You really are his son," the headmaster complimented.

"I would expect no less from a Tuatha Dé…" How much does he know? Maybe the royal family shared information to help the headmaster keep the hero in check.

"Uh, Lugh. I'm not really following this. Can you tell me what's happening?" Dia asked.

"The hero is the strongest living thing in the world. His power defies all norms. No one can hope to restrain the hero with strength alone. If the hero decided to destroy the Alvanian Kingdom, the country would be finished. Do you get it now?" I asked.

"Yeah, I understand. That strength could be a problem," Dia replied.

"Right. An unfettered hero is scarier than even the monsters and their master, the Demon King. That's why we need to reach his heart. To put it simply, if Epona has good friends, that will make him want to protect the country. The hero doesn't need support. Companions would only slow him down in a fight. What we are being asked to do is observe him and become the chains binding his heart."

"No way…"

The hero was so strong that drugs wouldn't have any effect on him. Brainwashing was unlikely to work, either. That's why we needed to become his friends and appeal to his emotions. It was cruel, but it made sense.

"Hmm, I have nothing to add. It is all as Lugh said. Whether you think you can do it or not, I want you to try. In a way, you'll be offering a service to Alvan greater than even the hero himself. You can expect a suitable reward," the headmaster assured us.

Tarte's shoulders had begun to shake. She looked like she was going to say something, though she remained quiet. I met her eyes and urged her to speak, and she timidly raised a hand.

"U-um, what would happen if this conversation were to leak outside of this room?"

"It would be treason against the kingdom—treason of the highest order. Failing at this task would end in the same result," the headmaster responded coolly.

He was saying that the four of us and all others involved would receive capital punishment. If Tarte were to be accused of sedition, my parents and I would also be executed.

Naoise and I made eye contact, and we both forced a smile. This was quite a responsibility to heap upon a group of fourteen-year-olds.

"Understood. Let's become Epona's dearest friends," Naoise declared.

"I will do my best to make that happen," I said.

"Looks like we don't have a choice. Count me in, too," added Dia.

"I'll do my best! I follow Lord Lugh wherever he goes!" Tarte vowed.

And so the four of us were given the duty of becoming the hero's companions. Thankfully, the academy seemed prepared to assist us to some extent.

The school was using me, and I was using the school. In a way, it was the best form of cooperation I could've hoped for.

We left the headmaster's office to find a large, kind-looking male professor waiting for us with a smile.

"Hey, it looks like the headmaster is finally finished with you. Come to the dining hall; there's a welcome party being held there for the new students. You don't want to miss out on the feast! Naoise and Lugh, I would like you two to give a speech greeting the new students. Think it over for me."

In an instant, the gloomy mood of the previous conversation had been wiped away.

"I'm not particularly good at that kind of thing," said Naoise.

"Oh, get out of here, Naoise. There's no way you're bad at public speaking," I shot back.

"You got me... Back to the previous topic. You and I should be able to accomplish anything together. All we have to do is manipulate a kid who's scared of other people and lacks confidence. That should be nothing for us."

"For sure. Looking at it like that, it doesn't sound too hard."

"Ha-ha-ha, and suddenly we're working together. This isn't so bad. I'm looking forward to seeing what you can do."

We walked to the welcome party without another word.

I couldn't help but worry about that future the goddess had told me about, though.

Once the hero defeats the Demon King, they will go insane and bring the world to ruin.

...What exactly *is going to cause that future to come about?*

If Naoise and I become the hero's friends and he goes mad anyway, then we might be the cause of that instability. Perhaps he's destined to lash out at the world after discovering our betrayal.

I was likely overthinking things, but it was undeniable that our little quartet was a group of traitors. Naoise had his own goals he was working toward, and I was only ingratiating myself with the hero so I could kill him one day.

We owed it to Epona to at least try to make him happy, even if our friendship was a sham. If we could succeed in doing that, maybe we could find a future where he didn't lose his mind. That way, I wouldn't have to kill him.

When we reached the feast hall, I spotted Epona, clearly alone despite the flock of people surrounding him.

Time to introduce myself to him. I need to make sure I leave a good impression.

A party was being held in the dorm's dining hall to celebrate the new students' arrival. It was a magnificent feast, complete with alcohol.

"Hey, this food isn't bad," said Dia.

"Naoise probably eats this kind of food every day," I remarked.

Given the liveliness, the banquet had clearly started before our arrival.

A large crowd of students encircled Epona.

If I had approached him before the entrance exam, he would've thought of me as just another face in a giant swarm of people trying to force themselves into his life. Now that I was the head of the class, however, I would stand out.

The crowd parted as I approached Epona.

I'd been observing him this entire time. I'd watched his every move intently during the exam. For that reason, I knew exactly how to deal with him.

All right, time for first contact.

"I'm your classmate, Lugh Tuatha Dé. It's nice to meet you."

"N-nice to meet you, too. I'm u-uh, Epona. Epona Rhiannon."

Epona squeezed my outstretched hand tightly.

His skin was calloused. It wasn't the sort that came about from regular sword practice like you might've expected the child of a distinguished military family to have, however. It was the kind that came from agricultural work. His muscles also betrayed the build of a farmer. He really didn't seem to have much combat experience.

"We're going to be in the same class, so we should be friends. Let's do our best to support each other," I said with a smile.

"O-okay. But I don't think I have anything I can teach you—"

"There's no need for modesty. You're very gifted physically. There's a lot I would like to learn from you."

"R-really? Then can you please teach me how to study? I didn't understand anything on the exam."

"Sure, I'd be happy to help."

I spoke to him cheerfully, and our conversation began to pick up steam. I thought it best not to be overly formal. Epona may have been the hero, but I knew he didn't want that.

He'd known only cruelty most of his life, but once he became the hero, he was quickly subjected to nothing but the highest flattery. He was alone growing up, and becoming the hero had done little to change that. It was clear to me that Epona was starved for the warmth of human affection.

That's why he looked so lonely despite being surrounded by so many people.

What Epona wanted was someone who'd converse with him as an equal, and that's what I was aiming to provide.

Eventually, the flow of our conversation changed. Initially, Epona was only responding to things I said, but he began to take the initiative and introduce topics himself after a little while. That was proof he was opening his heart to me. I thought it wise to withdraw soon.

I wanted to leave him only with favorable memories of me but still wanting more. He needed to be reluctant to see me go.

Just then, a professor approached me. It was time for me to deliver my address as a representative of the new students.

"Sorry, Epona. It looks like I have to go," I said remorsefully.

"That's okay. You're head of the class, so it can't be helped. It's amazing you were able to achieve so much despite being from a baron's family like me."

I thought I saw a flash of envy in Epona's eyes.

"I can't say that birth is irrelevant, but it isn't everything," I replied.

"You're amazing, Lugh. You're so mature, daring, and cool. Also, if I have you…it seems like you won't get hurt."

Epona said that last part in a barely audible whisper. I probably wouldn't have heard it without my enhanced hearing.

"It seems like you won't get hurt." What did he mean by that?

Naoise and I moved to a location in the dining hall where we would stand out the most and gathered all the new students' attention.

Naoise spoke first.

"I don't feel like dragging this out, so I'm just going to say what is foremost on my mind. I want to compete with every one of you. The growth I will gain contending with you all is the main reason I came to this academy. Force me to improve by threatening my spot as head of the class! Let's all strive to get stronger together. That is all I have to say."

After his extremely manly speech ended, the students erupted in applause.

Well, isn't he cool? That's not going to be easy to follow up.

Naoise gave me a mischievous look. Clearly, he'd given me a tough act to follow on purpose.

His words hadn't been a lie, though, so I couldn't be mad at him for it. Nothing he'd said had been merely to rile everyone up.

All right, I need to focus on my speech. I'm up next.

"Every one of us left our homes behind to come here. Honestly, two years is a long time, and I'm sure there are plenty of us who would rather have devoted this time to developing our own domains," I began.

A good number of people laughed.

"Even still, we were summoned here to pledge our allegiance to the Alvanian Kingdom. I swear to you that your time here will not be a waste and that you will gain a lot during your tenure at this school. I want everyone to think of it that way, because this country's prosperity depends on our growth. Let's all do our best so that two years from now, we'll look back and be glad we came here."

Dia and Tarte clapped loudly, and then applause spread through the rest of the crowd like a chain reaction. My speech was pretty corny, but it was perfect for the sort of situation I was in.

A professor gave some closing words, and Naoise and I returned to the party. Dia and Tarte wasted no time in approaching.

"Lugh, that was so cool," praised Dia.

"Yes, your speech was so grand. You really felt like the head of the class! It's a shame there isn't a spell that can preserve sound," Tarte said.

"Thanks. It was a little embarrassing, though," I replied.

"By the way, I picked out some food I thought you might like since you haven't had a chance to eat yet, my lord. Here you go."

Tarte handed me a plate with a few different items arranged neatly on it. Just as she'd said, it was all stuff I liked, and she'd even gotten me perfect portions of each.

"You're a lifesaver, Tarte. There's barely any food left. Guess that's to be expected with so many growing teenagers in one place," I stated.

"So how did things go with our job tonight?" asked Dia.

"Good. I made contact with Epona. A lot of the people hanging around him are looking at me now. I broke off our conversation at the perfect time, so I expect him to approach me before long."

I took a moment to look around and noticed someone walking toward me.

Then I caught sight of Naoise speaking with Epona. He was going for a different sort of approach to get close to the hero.

He's skilled at this, I thought. The higher ranking a noble was, the greater the need to know how to deal with their superiors. The highest members of the aristocracy received special education from a young age for this purpose. I held no doubts that Naoise was perfectly capable.

One thing was bothering me, however. Naoise was talking to Epona as if the hero was a girl. Epona was officially a boy. I needed to look into the matter again. Naoise was the son of a duke. Perhaps he was privy to more information on the hero than I was.

"Dia, Tarte. On the surface, your social status means nothing here. But…," I started.

"I understand, Lugh. I know that's not how people think," Dia affirmed.

"I'll do my best not to shame you, my lord," added Tarte.

So long as they understand, we'll be fine.

A Class S boy from a notable family of knights sauntered up to me. I wanted to make sure I was on good terms with him.

After the welcome party ended, everyone was guided to their assigned dormitories.

"It's weird to me that there are three different kinds of lodgings," remarked Dia.

"It would be much less of a hassle if there were only one. I'll never understand how rich people think," Tarte agreed.

They were both puzzled as to why there were multiple places where students could live.

"There's a reason the domiciles are divided. You'll understand when we get there," I stated.

The first dorm was only for Class S students and their servants. When we arrived at our assigned place of stay, Tarte's eyes went wide.

"This isn't a dormitory. This is a mansion!" she exclaimed.

"Students are treated entirely differently depending on what class they're in. That doesn't just apply to our lessons; it also extends to our lifestyle," I said.

Once inside, we were each assigned our own quarters. Dia had rooms separate from mine, but since Tarte was my servant, she would be staying in the same suite as I was.

We had a living room, a kitchen, and three other all-purpose rooms. Our furniture and decorations were all top-rate items of the highest quality. Apparently, the school was even prepared to supply us with more furniture if we desired. Even our laundry was handled by academy staff.

"So this is our apartment, my lord." Tarte marveled at the place.

"Sorry about this, Tarte. Servants are given a room in their master's quarters. Your grade was good enough to enter Class S as a student. You could've had one of these apartments to yourself," I said.

"I'm not unhappy about this at all! I'm glad we're together. Sharing a room with you, my lord... We've been living in the same house for years now, but for some reason, I feel really nervous about it."

Tarte suddenly clenched her fists tightly in front of her chest, and her breathing grew heavy. She was scaring me a bit.

There was a knock at the door, and I answered it.

"Lugh, Tarte hasn't flung herself on you yet, has she?" Dia asked, peeking in.

"Wh-what are you saying?!" Tarte cried.

"Hmm-hmm, I'm sure sharing an apartment between just the two of you is making you feel uneasy. Maybe I should live here, too. There are enough rooms for us each to have our own."

"But what will you do about your room, Dia?" I asked.

"I'll use it for storage. It's the perfect size for it," she replied.

Spoken like a true noble who had spent their entire life in a castle.

"Are you serious?" I pressed.

"Of course I am. I'm fine with you forming that kind of relationship with Tarte, but I don't like the idea of her getting a head start on me," Dia replied evenly.

"I–I'm going to do no such thing! I'm not that daring!" Tarte exclaimed.

I was tempted to ask Tarte what she would do if she was a little more daring, but that would be stepping on a land mine.

"Anyway, I don't mind you living here, Dia. You can move in if you like," I said.

"I'm okay with it, too. It will be easier to take care of you this way. Honestly, this is a relief. If it had been just Lugh and me, I would've… *Ahem*." Tarte left that last part unspoken.

"All right, I'll get my luggage later," Dia decided.

We would still have our own rooms in my quarters, so I didn't foresee a problem.

…Though if my classmates hear I'm living with two cute girls, I'll get teased relentlessly. On paper, though, they're just my little sister and retainer.

"I'm shocked by how luxurious this dorm is. I can't believe they give this much space to one student. I guess that's to be expected of an academy built for mages, though," Tarte observed.

"Well, they only go this far for students in Class S. Class A students are given their own rooms, but their beds, desks, and dressers take up most of the space. Those in Class B and down have to share a room with a roommate, and they have no choice but to either do their chores or have their servants do them. That's why everyone works so hard preparing for the exams. It's the only way to get into a higher class and live more comfortably."

I thought it to be a perfect motivation. The pupils in the lower classes would undoubtedly study their best so they could get their own rooms.

"Wait a second, what about the students in Class B and lower who have servants? How do their servants take care of them?" Dia inquired.

"All servants who are not in Class S stay in Class C's dorm in shared rooms designated for servants. They then travel between that dorm and their master's dorm."

"That means if my grades drop, I'll be separated from you... That would be terrible. I'll do my best so we can continue living together, my lord!" Tarte declared.

"I don't like the sound of that, either. I'll make sure to give it my all, too," Dia added.

"You shouldn't need that kind of short-term goal to want to study," I muttered with a forced smile. In Tarte's case, her place of residence depended entirely on my grades, so she didn't need to study. I liked her enthusiasm, however, so I held my tongue.

"You're right! I still can't get over how incredible this place is. We even have a kitchen. I can use it for baking a cake to celebrate Lord Lugh becoming head of the class," Tarte said, enthused.

"Let's leave the cake for after training. There's a work-out room in the Class S dorm. You can make reservations, so I'll be able to use it to teach you both Tuatha Dé techniques," I replied.

"We have everything we could ever want here. All right, leaving the cake for after a workout sounds good. It'll taste even better that way," Dia decided.

"I agree. I'm going to be studying and training with Lord Lugh and then sleeping in the same apartment every night. This makes me feel bad for Maha," admitted Tarte.

Maha was probably working hard at the store right now. I'd have to give her a request to perform a follow-up investigation into Epona. I needed to learn everything there was to know about House Rhiannon.

Dia, Tarte, and I headed to the training room. I was taken aback by the variety of equipment and the spaciousness of the place.

It looked like our new life at school was going to be quite comfortable.

Chapter 8 | The Assassin Goes to Class

After exercising in the workout room, I took a shower and returned to the apartment.

Before I went to sleep, I took a moment to reflect on the day's training.

I had succeeded in creating a new killing move. It was a trick that involved the Leather Crane Bag. The maneuver still had room for improvement, but I was happy to have the basic idea down.

Dia had finally established a foundational level of physical strength. Her prior sword training helped her learn the basics in a short amount of time. I planned to move her onto practical training soon. It's fair to say her training was progressing quite smoothly.

The problem was Tarte.

"...As I feared, her swiftness is becoming too much for her vision."

Tarte could fight at ridiculous speeds thanks to her training in the Tuatha Dé methods. Her superior physical strengthening technique and the acceleration of her wind affinity also played a part. Unfortunately, her eyes weren't able to keep up anymore.

She'd be fine against most elite-level opponents, but if her opponent was as strong as my dad or me, she'd go down easily.

There were a few ways to fix this.

The first was to train Tarte to only fight at a pace her senses could keep up with. That was the simplest solution, but it'd also limit her power.

The second method was to give her Tuatha Dé eyes. They would dramatically increase her perception.

My dad had already taught me how to perform the surgery. I needed to practice on someone before I did the procedure on my future child anyway.

But if I failed, it would mean blindness for Tarte.

I at least wanted some kind of practice before attempting the surgery on Tarte. I'd done the operation many times on criminals, but it'd failed on almost all the non-mages. That really only served as a way to memorize the steps in the procedure.

To be absolutely safe, I wanted a mage to rehearse on.

"Next time I get an assassination job, I'll secure the target for that."

It seemed the best way for me to get what I wanted. I'd report that I'd killed the target, but instead, I'd kidnap them, practice implanting the Tuatha Dé eyes, then kill them.

The biggest problem with that plan was I wasn't going to have many assassination opportunities while at the academy. My dad was handling requests while I was away. The only exception would be a target at the school itself. My dad was sure to hand such marks over to me.

A bell sounded in every dormitory, signifying that it was time to wake up. I changed into my uniform, left my room, and went to the living room.

I looked at my reflection in the mirror.

My uniform was black with a blue outline. I had an armband garnished with the golden symbol of Class S. The armband was a quick indicator of which class a student was in and determined the treatment they'd receive at the facilities throughout the academy.

"Good morning, my lord."

"Morning, Tarte. Your uniform looks cute on you."

"It fits me well and is really easy to move in. I like it, too."

Tarte gave a spin, her skirt fluttering in the air.

Her outfit was somewhere between a maid's attire and a school uniform. The servants' clothes had a different design so you could tell them apart from the students.

"I think I like yours better. It's cuter than mine," Dia said sleepily, rubbing her eyes as she entered the room.

Dia's garb possessed a more elegant appearance. It hugged close to her slender frame.

"You think so? I think that uniform definitely suits you better, Lady Dia," Tarte complimented.

"I agree. You look even better in beautiful clothes like that than you do in cute ones," I added.

"…You're making me blush. But I'm happy. It's good that Tarte and I both have outfits that suit us so well," replied Dia.

I couldn't have agreed more, just like how more elegant attire suited Dia, cuter garb befitted Tarte.

"You two haven't forgotten anything, have you? The first day is critical," I cautioned.

"Have a little faith in me, Lugh," Dia said back.

"I checked multiple times yesterday, so I'm fine…," Tarte answered. "Okay, breakfast is ready."

Tarte brought plates of food into the living room. The main dish was corn soup. She had also made freshly baked bread with lettuce and soft scrambled eggs placed on top. I had some of those after spreading Tarte's special tomato sauce on them.

"Where'd you get these ingredients?" I asked.

"Last night, someone came to our dorm and asked me if we wanted them to supply us with ingredients to make breakfast or if we'd use the dining hall. I asked for ingredients, and they were delivered this morning," Tarte explained.

"Good decision. Your cooking puts me at ease. I haven't been able to relax since yesterday, so I'm grateful," I replied.

"Yeah, I want to eat with just the three of us every day. This is better than eating at the dining hall," Dia agreed.

We ended up having a lovely, laid-back meal. We enjoyed some black tea and leftovers from the cake Tarte had baked last night after we finished eating. Before we knew it, the exhaustion from yesterday was gone.

As soon as we left the dorm, Naoise rushed over to join us.

"Good morning, Tuatha Dé. What do you say to heading to class together?"

"Good morning. Sure, let's go," I said.

"Ha-ha-ha. It turns out even I am prone to feelings of help-lessness when alone. I had quite an unfortunate incident this morning," Naoise revealed.

"You did?" I asked.

"Yes. I decided to get breakfast in the dining hall. Unbe-knownst to me, the seat I chose turned out to be designated for upperclassmen, so I got a good telling off. They were nice enough to let me remain there because it's the first day, though."

Our dormitory was for Class S students. That included upper-class students, so what Naoise was describing was possible.

"This rigid system of seniority is annoying. We should be careful of older students going forward," I said.

"I guess. Some of our seniors seemed easy enough to get along with, so I'll see if I can't extract some useful info from them," Naoise answered with a laugh.

Naoise had also brought a servant to the academy. He could've just as easily taken his meals in his room. He'd probably decided to eat in the dining hall because he wanted to build connections. I was willing to bet he'd sat at that upper-class student table specifically to make an impression.

"Just make sure you don't go too far," I chided.

"...Wow, you get it, don't you? Since that's a warning from a dear friend, I'll be sure to be careful," replied Naoise.

It took about three minutes of walking to arrive at our classroom building. We'd come about ten minutes before lessons began, but everyone else was already there.

There were three significant people in my classroom: Naoise Gephis, eldest son of the dukedom of Gephis; Finn MacCool, the second son of House MacCool, a lineage known for their knights; and the hero Epona Rhiannon. Everyone else was excellent in their own regard, but not to the point where I needed to give them special attention.

It was best not to get on the wrong side of Naoise or Finn. They both held high social standings, and most importantly, they were capable combatants.

Finn trumped me in terms of pure swordsmanship. The

sharpness of his mind was not to be discounted, either. He'd seemed quiet when I talked to him at the party last night, but his intelligence was apparent. While he didn't flaunt his ability like Naoise, I needed to be careful around him all the same.

"Good morning." I greeted my classmates with a smile, and everyone welcomed me back. On the surface, at least, it seemed no one in Class S held animosity toward me because I was the son of a baron.

Naoise said a couple of words to me and then walked toward Finn. He'd undoubtedly noticed Finn's skill and was probably planning on acquiring him just as he was with me.

Before long, the professor arrived. The bell rang as he walked through the door.

"Looks like you're all here. I'll begin by introducing myself. I am your instructor for this class, Miles Dune."

Like most of the instructors at the academy, Miles Dune had a well-toned body. He was a dark-skinned man with a robust physique, keen eyes, and a presence that suggested he'd seen plenty of combat.

"Every one of you has an ability that separates you from the rest of the first-year students at this school...for now. That could all change in as little time as six months."

Half a year. That's when the next exam would be held. Students were moved up and down into the different classes based on the tests held throughout our academy tenure.

"With the favorable treatment you're all receiving, I bet none of you think you'll ever lose your spots in Class S. In a way, that's correct...but don't underestimate the tenacity of those trying to claw their way up to your current positions. Every assessment period changes the roster. I recommend you all find a sense of urgency. Otherwise, you might find yourselves booted from Class S sooner than you think."

So even though we've succeeded in getting into Class S, we still have to study like maniacs to stay in it.

"Now that the preamble is out of the way, let's get started with your first lesson. During your two years here, you will gain the education and strength necessary to serve the Alvanian Kingdom effectively... There is one other thing I forgot to mention. You all have obtained the best circumstances possible for your growth. I want you to conduct yourselves appropriately, as Class S is the face of this academy."

The students nodded, and the first lesson of the year commenced.

We began with Alvanian history. After looking at the other students, I noticed that Epona had his head in his hands. I made a mental note to strike up a conversation with him later by offering to help him study.

Suddenly, I sensed a familiar presence.

I looked out the window and saw a white pigeon flying by.

It was a special messenger bird used by House Tuatha Dé, and it was flying toward my room.

The only ones who contacted me that way were my dad and Maha. It was rare for my dad to send a missive, and I'd only sent Maha the request for an additional investigation into Epona yesterday. Maha was superbly talented, but there's no way she could've sent results back already, so it must've been something else.

...I'll go check that right after class.

If my dad sent the message, then it was probably an urgent assassination job. If Maha was contacting me, then chances were it was regarding some troublesome matter that she and the older brother of my fake identity couldn't deal with alone.

My classes were done. Our first day at school had mostly just been lectures.

"Hey, Lugh, want to get lunch at the café? The members of Class S should build a sense of unity," said Naoise.

"Sorry, I can't today. Please invite me next time, though."

I understood how building intimacy with my classmates was essential, but I needed to check the contents of that letter as soon as possible.

"That's too bad."

"If Lugh isn't going, then I'm gonna head back to the dorm, too," Dia declared, and Tarte nodded.

"No, you two should go. It would look bad if none of us went, so can you both go and represent House Tuatha Dé for me?" I asked.

I wanted to avoid the three of us isolating ourselves here. If they went with the others, they could create some connections.

"Okay, I understand. You should do your part to get close to everyone, too, Lugh."

Dia had grown up the daughter of a count, so she was used to the nobility's politics. I didn't need to spell this kind of thing out for her.

I smiled at Tarte, who was looking anxious, and then I returned to the dorm.

The carrier pigeon was resting its wings in our apartment's bird-cage. The little creature had a letter tied to one of its legs.

"You must've worked really hard to get here. You did a good job," I said, petting the bird.

I took the message and opened it.

"It's from Dad. Not sure if that's a good or a bad thing."

He was just asking how things were going at the academy, if I was watching my diet, and if I needed any money.

This is a code. There's no way he would use a carrier pigeon to send that kind of missive.

When using a carrier pigeon, there was a risk of an intercept and information leaking. For that reason, the letter was encoded so that if a third party read it, it would just seem like the simple message of a dad worried about his son. The cryptic dispatch would raise suspicion if the content didn't make any sense.

I got to work on decoding the note.

"…I see, that's why he contacted me."

After reading all the way through, I laughed.

Apparently, an assassin had infiltrated the academy to assassinate the hero, Epona. I needed to find that assassin and kill them. The headmaster had already been informed and could provide me with backup. There was no information about the killer, so I first needed to identify them.

"I need to protect Epona? What kind of joke is this? Like any assassin would actually be able to kill him. Just let them try."

From the moment I'd laid eyes on Epona, I'd been thinking about how to off him. Unfortunately, I'd still yet to come up with an answer. Even if I were to catch him completely off guard, it would've been nearly impossible.

In my mind, I imagined how best to end Epona if he warmed up to me and approached in a vulnerable state. Even then, I could only see my attempts ending in failure.

As of right now, the attack with the highest probability of killing him was Gungnir. And even that would take more than one shot.

I could've launched multiple god spears into the sky for as long as my mana would hold and then carpet-bombed Epona while he was sleeping. By my estimation, however, even that plan would've only had about a 20 percent chance of getting the job done.

Who is this idiot who thinks they're going to be able to kill him?

"...Whatever, I'll look for them."

Perhaps Epona had some weak point I didn't know about.

Despite being tasked with assassinating the hero, it now fell to me to protect him. How ironic.

Later that evening, we went to the workout room. I was currently performing a mock battle with Tarte.

Tarte accelerated using both her physical strengthening and her wind affinity.

I used the same trick. I was the one who taught her the tactic, so I could do it, too.

We were moving at about the same speed. There was a clear difference forming between us, however. It was one born of our eyes. Tarte was unable to register my actions clearly, but I could see everything she was doing perfectly. She didn't have a chance.

The fight ended after about thirty seconds when I knocked her spear down.

"I knew I wouldn't be able to beat you, my lord..."

"No, you're doing well. I have an unfair advantage."

"Is it your eyes? ...I'm jealous."

"Tarte, do you want a pair of these eyes?"

I did think it best that Tarte had them, but it might not have been what she wanted.

"Of course. If I have those eyes, I can be a greater help to you, and most importantly, it'll ensure that I can be with you forever."

"If you truly want them, then I think it would be okay to give them to you. But you should know there is a small risk of blindness if the surgery fails. I want you to think about that before you make a decision."

"I don't need to think about it. I want them anyway. There's no way you'll fail, my lord, and even if you do, I'll have no regrets."

"...There's no way I can let myself fail after hearing you say that. I can't betray your trust."

Tarte said she would have no regrets even if the operation failed. Whatever I did, didn't want to be the cause of her losing her sight.

...That's it! Once I find the assassin going after Epona, I can experiment on them until I'm satisfied I can safely perform the surgery. Anyone entrusted with the job of killing the hero must surely have been a powerful mage. I would kill them anyway, so there was no harm in getting some use out of them first.

"Hey, Lugh. I have a suggestion. When you do the procedure, what about taking it one eye at a time? If the first eye goes well, then you can move on to the next. That way, worst-case scenario, she'll only go blind in one eye," Dia suggested.

"Good idea. That's what I'll do," I agreed.

"Lord Lugh, when are you going to do the surgery?" Tarte asked me, her eyes sparkling. This girl believed in me from the bottom of her heart.

"Please try not to think about it too much; it might not be until a month from now. I have some preparation I need to do first," I replied.

If I can just capture the assassin, then I'll be able to practice.

"I'm so excited… But are you sure it's okay for me to have those eyes? They're one of the Tuatha Dé clan's most closely guarded secrets."

"I don't mind at all. You're family, Tarte. And this isn't just hypothetical. I have permission from Dad. He says I can do as I like as long as I take appropriate responsibility."

Tarte had been serving me since we were little. She wasn't some simple retainer.

"Huh?! Family? Responsibility? I, um, whaaa—?"

Tarte's ears flushed red, and she looked down at the floor.

"…I didn't mean it like that. And I definitely want to avoid a situation where I have to take responsibility."

The responsibility I was talking about was how I'd have to kill Tarte if she betrayed me after I gave her the Tuatha Dé eyes.

"O-okay, I understand. I understand fully."

She was adorable when she got riled up.

For a moment, I thought about becoming family in the way that Tarte imagined. It was a nice idea.

Our first week at school had passed without incident. Combat practice was beginning. The assassin after Epona hadn't made a move yet.

We were currently performing one-on-one mock battles, with students being matched up based on their strength. Everyone was fighting with blunted weapons, and the use of magic was allowed.

Tarte's match ended, and she exited the ring. She didn't fight a servant, but rather the fifth-ranked student in the class, and beat her opponent handily.

"How did I do?"

"You handled the spear skillfully. You did make several mistakes, though. First..."

Tarte listened with a serious expression. Her ability to patiently listen to feedback and learn from it was her greatest weapon.

While I was talking to her, the match between Naoise, a skilled swordsman, and Finn, a young man from a long line of knights, began.

The entire class was entranced. Their match was a pure sword fight, which made it splendid to watch. Naoise won in the end, but it felt like it could've gone either way.

Next, my turn arrived.

Combat pairs were chosen based on each student's fighting prowess. Naoise, Finn, Dia, Tarte, and all the other highest-ranking students had already had their turns.

This left only one possible person who could be my partner.

"Next, Epona Rhiannon and Lugh Tuatha Dé."

Welp, it's Epona and me.

This was as good an opportunity as I could've asked for to observe the hero's strength firsthand—if I survived.

The commander of the Royal Order who had fought Epona during the exam was still bedridden. Despite receiving treatment from an elite healer, he still hadn't recovered.

The professor chose me to face Epona because he thought anyone else in the class would suffer the same fate. It was high praise, in a way.

"Um, Lugh, let's have a good match."

"Yeah, let's show the fruits of our training."

"I'm going to be careful, so please try not to get hurt."

"I'll do my best."

I gave the professor a look that said, *"Are you really making me do this?"* He just nodded in response.

"Are you two ready?"

"I'm good anytime," I replied.

"I'm ready, too," followed Epona.

I was using a blunted knife. I had no desire to use a sword. An accident was bound to happen if I didn't use the sort of weapon I was most comfortable with.

The professor raised his hand.

I immediately began to pour mana into my eyes. If I didn't power up my Tuatha Dé eyes to their limit—actually, past their limit—I wouldn't even be able to keep track of Epona's shadow. A sharp pain ran through my body due to the excessive strengthening, but I maintained this state by using Rapid Recovery to heal myself forcibly.

"Begin!"

Epona disappeared immediately. This was exactly what'd happened against the commander of the Royal Order.

The difference was that I had Tuatha Dé eyes.

I could follow Epona, but only barely. I stepped to the side and left my knife floating in the air. If I tried to attack the hero while still holding my weapon, my arm would probably break.

The ring cracked as Epona charged at me. My knife was blasted away faster than a speeding bullet, piercing a seat in the stands. I'd only barely managed to dodge Epona's attack, but I was knocked back about half a meter from the rush of air.

It was only barely visible, but a bruise formed on Epona's arm from hitting the knife.

The knife should have inflicted massive damage upon impact at that speed, but the hero's skin was unbelievably tough.

"…You dodged it. You evaded my attack. Just as I'd hoped, you're not going to get hurt."

Epona laughed. It was an innocent, joyful laugh from the bottom of his heart.

He then looked at me.

All right, I dodged his first attack, but what will he do next?

This may have been a practice bout, but my life was on the line nonetheless. Even so, I wanted to keep going.

Chapter 10 | The Assassin Gains the Hero's Confidence

After I avoided Epona's first attack, I glanced at the professor. Sure enough, that wasn't enough for him to call the match.

This mock battle was only going to end when a hit connected. Evidently, my knife bruising Epona's arm wasn't enough. Things would've completed painlessly if that had counted.

"Here I come!"

Epona charged at me with his next attack, his face flushed red with excitement. He seemed to be enjoying this fight. I was surprised. I didn't think he had that kind of personality.

Epona's greatest weapon was his ridiculous physical strength. That alone overwhelmed all the skills I'd spent years building up.

He wasn't without weakness, however. His preparatory movements for each attack were exaggerated and obvious, making it very easy to tell where he was aiming. He was also unskilled at moving his body, so it took him a bit to transition from one attack to the next.

Simply put, his strikes were too basic.

The more skilled a fighter you were, the more you realized that fights didn't always go as you expected. For that reason, you had to become able to read your opponent's moves, use feints, and adjust your movement throughout the fight.

Epona did none of that. The windup on everything he did was excessive, and every one of his movements betrayed his intent.

I dodged a second and third attack, getting more used to his pattern each time. Seeing the hero's speed and bad habits was incredibly valuable, and I was beginning to notice a few weak points.

The hero's physical ability defied all norms, and his ability to see objects in motion was also superhuman. But on that latter point, my Tuatha Dé eyes were even better. That was an important discovery. Unfortunately, such information was completely useless if I couldn't survive our sparring match.

"This is amazing! Why can't I hit you? You're slower than me!" Epona exclaimed.

My head felt like it was going to split. My brain was crying out from overuse. I'd only been able to evade because of how hard I was pushing myself. I wasn't going to be able to maintain this for much longer.

Every time I dodged a lethal attack, I erupted in sweat and felt like my life span was shortening.

Exhaustion was setting in. Rapid Recovery restored my stamina and mana, but its effect didn't replenish mental energy or concentration.

Even so, I fought to maintain my composure. Hasty choices weren't going to make the situation any better. They'd only provide Epona with a window to strike.

"What are you doing? You have to attack, Lugh. If you don't, then how could we even call this training?!"

I know that. But the moment I devote any of my energy to offense, my evasion will slip. If even a single blow connected, it could mean serious injury for me, regardless of how I defended against it. My only option was not to get hit at all.

I just have to last a little longer. My eyes were adjusting, and I'd memorized Epona's rhythm, habits, and attack pattern.

Epona was getting irritated. Each of his swings was getting more aggressive.

"Why...can't...I...hit...you?!"

His frustration was causing him to try to move even faster and force more power into his attacks. His motions were becoming more monotonous as a result.

Now that I'd pushed Epona to such a point, he was turning to his most effective attack. It was the same one he'd used to defeat the commander of the Royal Order: a simple step forward and uppercut.

Instead of reading his preparatory motion as I'd been doing, I made my move as soon as Epona entered his attack motion.

I saw this strike coming. Actually, that's not the most accurate way to put it. I'd forced Epona into this action. Understanding your opponent's habits and rhythm enabled you to guide their actions.

If I hadn't spent so long dodging the hero and reading his movements, I would never have been able to create the timing needed for a counter. That this kind of strategy could beat Epona was his greatest weakness.

...If you were to use this same tactic against an opponent of decent ability, they would've simply switched to a different pattern. Epona didn't have the experience or levelheadedness to do that. Even though I moved before he'd even started his attack, he rushed recklessly at me, swinging his fist upward.

I barely managed to remain outside the range of his fist, waited for his arm to extend, and then responded. At the beginning of the match, I'd only been able to get Epona to punch one of my knives, but this time, I brought my weapon down on him.

The blade made a dull breaking sound, and I was immediately blasted out of the ring from the air pressure of Epona's attack.

Unable to angle myself for a graceful landing, I hit the ground multiple times before I came to a stop.

...I guess this is what'll happen if I try to hit the hero head-on. I got blown out of the ring despite being the one to land the blow. It was absurd.

"Lugh wins!"

The professor had watched closely and noticed that I'd scored a valid strike before I'd gone flying, so he awarded me the victory.

"Lord Lugh, that was incredible!" Tarte praised.

"Wow, I can't believe you were able to defeat the hero!" Dia agreed.

"I already thought very highly of him, but even I didn't expect this. Finn, do you feel like you could do what he just did?" Naoise asked.

"Don't be ridiculous. I wouldn't have confidence in my ability to dodge Epona's attacks, much less land a counter... Lugh Tuatha Dé has incredible vision and the ability to read his opponent. I hate to admit this, but I would have no chance of beating the hero, and I don't think I could beat Lugh, either. What about you, Naoise?"

"I agree. That's why I want him. With you and him at my side, I could accomplish anything."

My classmates were chatting excitedly about my triumph.

...I somehow managed to win while concealing what exactly

had enabled my victory. My Tuatha Dé eyes enhanced my ability to see objects in motion, but that wasn't something an observer could've noticed at a distance.

I tried to get up and failed.

My breathing was ragged and my legs were shaking. Sweat had soaked me through. The fight had taken more out of me than I'd expected. I was exhausted more mentally than physically, however.

Just thinking about what would have happened if that had been a real battle was horrifying.

I was utterly spent, and the blow that won me the match had ended up cracking a bone in my arm. All Epona had to show for it was a light bruise on his forehead. I would have died if he'd grazed me with a single fist, but my counter barely damaged him at all. It was infuriating.

I have to kill him?

Epona walked over to me and held out a hand. I grabbed it, and he pulled me up.

"I'm glad I met you, Lugh. I want to fight with you again," Epona said.

With those words, my fear that he enjoyed fighting grew. An interest in fighting explained why Epona had said something as vaguely dangerous as, *"It seems like you won't get hurt."*

"I'm surprised. I didn't take you for the type who enjoys combat," I replied.

"It's not that I like it. I have to get stronger because I'm the hero and because I promised Mireille. I need to train as much as I can to fulfill that promise, but everyone I fight gets hurt. I want to become stronger, but I can't."

There weren't many people who could go toe to toe with Epona and survive, even if it was only a practice match.

"I've been anxious that I'm not going to be strong enough to defeat the demons. But because I can trust that you won't get hurt, Lugh, I can properly train. I won't even have to hold back when we practice. I can finally become stronger. So can you spar with me again sometime? You're all I have, Lugh!"

Epona's movements were probably so unskilled because he'd never been able to train correctly. There were many things you could only learn through actual battle experience, but Epona had never had anyone capable of showing him the way.

Evidently, he didn't have any particular love of violence, but felt obligated to improve because he was the hero. He'd also mentioned a vow to some person named Mireille. If I accepted Epona's request, then I'd become an irreplaceable presence in his life, and we'd develop a deep bond.

Unfortunately, it also meant risking my life. If I did this kind of thing repeatedly, my body wasn't going to last. What other choice did I have, though?

"I'd be glad to. I have plenty I can gain from it, too."

There was no doubt I would also get stronger through these life-threatening battles.

I'd be able to study the hero up close, and I'd grow stronger and gain his trust in the process. Such boons were worth risking my life.

"Okay, then I'll ask the professor to make you my opponent for all my mock battles!" Epona declared.

"Ha-ha-ha, that would be an honor. But it would be unfair to hog all the chances to fight the hero to myself. You all want to try fighting Epona, too, right?"

I looked to my classmates for help, but they all quickly turned away. That included Tarte and Dia. They all understood that even sparring with Epona was a life-and-death struggle.

"Looks like no one has a problem with it. I won't lose next time!" Epona said happily.

And just like that, I was going to be struggling for survival daily. I needed to mentally prepare myself for the likelihood of serious injury. I'd have to take great care to avoid any permanent damage.

Later that day, after classes ended, Epona begged me to help him with all the things he didn't understand. After that, I conducted Dia and Tarte's training and then finally returned to the apartment.

As I tutored Epona, I got the feeling he was relaxing more and more around me. Accepting his request had definitely been the right call.

After returning to my room, I sent a request to investigate the person the hero referred to as Mireille. My assassin's instinct was telling me they were the hero's biggest weakness. After that, I had Tarte undress, checked her body's condition, and then decided on her future training regimen.

A knock came at the door.

I looked at Tarte, and she hurriedly dressed herself and opened the door.

It was a boy with blond hair.

"Good evening, Lugh. You were marvelous today. I brought you a snack to thank you for putting on such a dazzling performance."

"Naoise. I'm exhausted, so would you mind leaving?"

"Ah-ha-ha-ha, come now, you don't need to treat me like that. I come with more than just this little gift. I have information you've been looking for."

"Is it about Epona?"

"That's right. She has a secret."

"...You said 'she.' So Epona *is* a girl."

Epona had been reported to be a boy and had entered the academy under that guise as well.

"You sound like you've been suspecting as much for a while," Naoise deduced.

"Epona's clothes disguise it, but her skeletal structure is female. Your interactions with her also gave it away. I've been trying to get close to Epona as a friend and equal, but you've been approaching Epona romantically," I stated.

"Ha-ha-ha, so you noticed that. Love would be the easiest way to get in her good graces. All you have to do with girls like her is show a little kindness, and they'll fall for you instantly."

Tarte glared at Naoise after he said that. She had a pure heart and didn't appreciate hearing that kind of thing.

"Tarte, darling, don't look at me like that. I'm not just toying with her. Any way I can win over the hero will get me closer to my goal. If we form a real romantic relationship, I'll stay with her until the end and love her with all my heart. I'm serious about that, even if I have an ulterior motive," assured Naoise.

"Really?" Tarte remained dubious.

"Am I correct to assume the reason you're sharing this with me is that your advances have proven difficult?" I probed.

"That's exactly right. You seem to have stolen her heart with your performance earlier... My plan would still be on if I could prove to her that I can also safely fight her. Unfortunately, I am not capable of that. I don't know how you were able to deal with her speed," Naoise admitted.

"Trust me, it wasn't easy," I answered.

"In any case, that will make romance difficult for me, so I've decided I should get close to her as your friend. This means the closer your relationship is with her, the better. Now, for the main topic. As for why she was raised as a boy…"

I listened carefully to Naoise's explanation. It turned out to be largely what I'd expected. There were few reasons to raise a noble-born girl as male.

"Thank you, Naoise. I think I'll be able to use this to get even closer to her," I stated.

"I'm glad I could be of help. All right, I'm leaving. This is probably too forward of me, but I recommend you don't get too familiar with her."

"I'll keep that in mind. Unlike you, I don't plan on approaching Epona romantically."

Keeping some amount of distance was probably the best decision. I didn't want the hero to get overly attached.

Tarte was visibly relieved after I'd said I didn't intend to court Epona. Not wanting to make her or Dia sad was one reason I didn't like the idea.

"Naoise, can I ask a favor? We have tomorrow off. I have something I need to take care of and won't be at the academy. Can you watch Epona for me?" I requested.

"You want me to keep an eye on her? Sure. I don't feel the slightest need to keep that promise, but I'll do it… In exchange, can I borrow Tarte for a day? I want to take her out for a date."

"If that's your condition for accepting the request, then no," I responded without hesitation. I would never use Tarte that way.

"That's disappointing. Let's pretend I was joking. Please don't be mad at me. I only mentioned that because I genuinely like Tarte. All right, I'll settle for you owing me one. I'm heading out." With that, Naoise made to leave.

"Thanks. Sorry for the imposition," I said.

My asking Naoise to watch Epona had possibly revealed more than I would've liked.

Under my dad's orders, I was cooperating with the school to deal with an assassin aiming for Epona's life. This was possible because the duke who knew the secret of House Tuatha Dé made certain preparations for us. The academy had likely told Naoise about things as well.

"Lord Lugh, um, thank you for that… I would have gone if you told me to. But I would have hated it, so I'm very happy you refused him for me," Tarte said shyly.

"Of course. You're an important member of our family, Tarte."

"…! I'll work even harder for you from now on, my lord!"

Tarte looked at me with fire in her eyes. I felt a little awkward, so I looked away and changed the subject.

"By the way, where is Dia? I haven't seen her since training," I mentioned.

"She said she had something she wanted to check at the library. After practice, she changed and went straight there."

"The library here is awe-inspiring. Okay, that's fine. I'll tell her later. I have a request for you, Tarte. Can you make a boxed lunch for our day off tomorrow? I'm thinking about going out for a picnic."

"Ah, that sounds nice. I'll make something special for us."

The innocuous outing would help Tarte and Dia de-stress while also enabling me to test the new, deadly technique I'd been working on. I hoped to also use the picnic as a method to trap the assassin after Epona.

The site of our little getaway was a secluded spot a short distance from a major road. There, I'd be able to make as much noise as I pleased without any unwanted attention.

Dia, Tarte, and I were headed off on our excursion. Tarte was walking cheerfully while carrying a basket full of food. She must have been looking forward to this, as she had woken up very early to prepare our lunch.

Conversely, Dia was in the middle of an exhausted yawn.

"You really stayed up late last night," I observed.

"Yeah, but I was finally able to finish it. I found the final piece I needed in a book I borrowed from the library... I'm so tired," Dia replied.

"Is this for a new spell?" I asked.

"Yeah. One you've been asking for. I've been working on complex and powerful spells for a while, but I've also been toying with the idea of creating magic that prioritizes speed. I compressed information as much as I could to create the shortest formulas possible. They aren't powerful, and they're pretty inaccurate, but they're quite quick and easy to use," Dia explained.

"That sounds helpful. Magic can be difficult to use in combat," I said.

When casting a spell, you needed to utter an incantation. Finding time to do that when someone was trying to kill you could be difficult. Outside of Wind Armor, there weren't many spells that were usable in a direct fight.

Wind Armor was one of Tarte's favorite bits of magic to use. The defensive enchantment would last for a while, so you could cast it before you ever engaged an enemy. Unfortunately, that wasn't the case with most other spells. Typically, sorcerers worked on incantations while a vanguard of infantry protected them.

I wanted to see if something could be done about that drawback, though. As such, Dia and I had been conducting some research. These shortened spells were the result.

I analyzed Dia's formula. The way she was able to compress the recipe down to such a small size was nothing short of art. She had such an incredible sense for magic. I never would've come up with something this brilliant.

"This is a good formula. I'll go ahead and use Spell Weaver to make it a new spell," I said.

"Hmm-hmm, it's only three lines. It shouldn't take more than a second to cast," Dia responded.

"For sure."

Dia and I regularly exercised our tongues to perform incantations at high speeds, and as such, we were capable of chanting much faster than the average person. A three-line recitation would only take us a single second. Perhaps even less.

"It's too bad it's a fire spell. That means I can't use it," Tarte admitted with dejection.

"You have Wind Armor, Tarte. Isn't that good enough?" I asked.

"I can use that in combat if I whisper the incantation beforehand, but after it wears off, I have no way of casting it again."

She had a point. Wind Armor was a powerful spell, and its necessary chant was proportionally long.

Tarte looked at Dia pleadingly.

"Okay fine, I'll make a wind formula for you. But in exchange, you have to bake another cake… I don't know how your cakes end up so delicious despite not using any expensive ingredients. You're not any more skilled than my pastry chef," said Dia.

"Um, maybe it's because I bake them with love?" Tarte posited.

"Why do you sound so unsure of that?" Dia questioned. She and Tarte both laughed. "Anyway, this mountain makes for a nice stroll. It's perfect for a picnic."

"Yes, the roads are maintained very well," agreed Tarte.

"That's because the army often marches through this area. It's taken good care of," I explained.

Climbing an undeveloped mountain was very difficult. I was grateful we had a clear path to follow.

"It gets a bit rough up ahead," I cautioned. "People don't often go beyond this point. There's a good spot through this forest trail."

"So that's why you said I shouldn't wear my servant clothes. If I were wearing that outfit, my skirt would get caught on everything."

"Yeah. What we've got on now is much easier to move in."

The three of us were wearing Tuatha Dé combat clothes with robes over them.

The garb didn't bare much skin, and it hugged tightly to the body. It was the perfect sort of thing to wear when hiking. After folding up our robes, we ventured into the forest.

I led, cutting down obtrusive branches along the way, and we arrived at our destination before long.

"Wow, that riverbed is so pretty. This place is spacious, and the sound of the water is relaxing," Tarte remarked.

"We can make as much noise as we want here," Dia observed.

"Yeah, that's why I chose it. How about we eat first?" I said.

"Okay, I'll take out the food." Tarte spread out a sheet and opened the basket.

Our entrée was a large meat pie. When we cut into it, ample, creamy meat sauce with ground beef spilled out. It looked delicious.

Lunch had ended. Tarte's cooking had been just as tasty as it had looked.

"Oh yeah, Lugh. Is it okay that you're not watching her today?"

Dia was talking about Epona. I'd told both her and Tarte about the assassin.

"You saw our mock battle, right? There's no way anyone is even capable of killing her. Also, I asked Naoise to look after her. Epona doesn't really need a protector, but my leaving the academy today is actually a trap. If all goes according to plan, I'll have the assassin."

I'd been investigating ever since I'd learned that someone was aiming for Epona's life. I'd managed to catch traces of the assassin's presence here and there, but they'd seemed content to observe from a distance thus far. They were cautious. Hopefully, by presenting them with an opportunity, I could lure them into pouncing.

"If you're sure you've thought it all out, then I guess that's okay," Dia said.

"Of course."

As I'd already made clear, there was no reason to think Epona would die.

"All right, let's get started. I wrote down that spell, Dia. Go ahead and try to use it," I instructed.

"Okay. This is a rapid-fire spell that can be used from point-blank range... Watch this."

Dia spoke the incantation.

"Instant Flame!"

Fire burst forth less than a second after she began chanting. The blaze was extremely hot thanks to the powerful mana she'd cast it with. The heat was easily intense enough to kill.

"Okay, so it just shoots a jet of fire. It diffuses quickly, though, because the flames don't converge, but you can use it almost immediately. Its force also increases the more mana you use," explained Dia.

"It looks convenient. You could use it from any position," I remarked.

It was perfect for when you'd lost your balance in a sword fight and didn't have time to avoid the next oncoming attack. No opponent would expect such a quick spell. There was no limit to the kind of situations you could use it in, provided your opponent was unaware of the maneuver, of course.

"You've created something exceedingly useful, Dia," I complimented.

I tested Instant Flame for myself. Not only was it simple to utilize, but it could also create quite the blaze if you put all your mana into it. While its short range was a definite hindrance, the spell's versatility more than made up for that.

"Seeing you both use it makes me want magic like that even more. If this were a wind spell, I'd be able to blow away my opponent, gather myself, and then accelerate instantly. It would be even more useful than fire," Tarte stated.

I agreed with her. While a wind version would share some overlap with Wind Armor, the instant casting time would make a huge difference.

"All right, I'll make you a wind one. I won't be able to use it, but it sounds like it would serve you and Lugh well," Dia acknowledged. "That's all I have to reveal today. You're up next, Lugh."

"Okay. Time to unveil a new killing move... I've thought a lot about how to make use of my Leather Crane Bag. In the end, I kept coming back to the idea that it lets me carry around as many weapons as I want. As an example, think about Gun Strike. Forming the gun, loading it with bullets, and casting the explosion spell takes a long time," I began.

"Yeah, if you use that bag, you can carry around a pre-prepared gun. That will cut down on the casting time. That's kinda boring for you, though," Dia said.

"If that were all, it would be. But like I said, I can carry as many weapons as I want. Which means I can do this."

I severed the mana flowing into the magic bag. The alternate space within the bag immediately collapsed, and all of the contents burst out at once.

What erupted out of the bag were twenty guns as large as tank cannons, the kind I used not for Gun Strike, but Cannon Strike. If I didn't have to worry about each one's size, I could make them as big and powerful as I wanted. By increasing the number of them, I could also crank up the force of the attack.

Each barrel was loaded with bullets and shards of Fahr Stones. I'd adjusted the stones' size because the cannon cylinders weren't able to handle full-size ones. Every Fahr Stone was filled to the brim with mana and rang with the sound that signaled they were about to explode.

I then finished the incantation I'd been performing.

"Arrange!"

Using a magnetic force field, I shifted the direction of all twenty cannons. They all began to rumble, fixed in place in midair. Dia and Tarte knew by now to cover their ears and open their mouths.

"Cannon Volley!"

All of the weapons discharged simultaneously, reducing the shore by the river to ash. A single Cannon Strike couldn't compare to this level of destruction.

It was a successful test.

I had made one miscalculation, however. After the cannons fired in midair, the recoil proved too much for them to stay in place, and they were all sent flying backward.

The attack was definitely too dangerous to use in a situation where there were allies behind me. I needed to either set the cannons in the ground or somehow configure them to fire without any recoil. That was a problem for later, however.

"This is the killing move I've devised by experimenting with the Leather Crane Bag. With it, I can fire dozens of Cannon Strikes at the same time. I call it Cannon Volley," I said.

It was a bombardment of shots; every one of them held the power of a tank behind it. Best of all, it hardly took any time to cast. It was a worthy addition to my deadly arsenal.

"What the hell are you planning on using this for?! You wouldn't need this much firepower to kill a dragon!" Dia exclaimed.

"It really doesn't seem to be a spell meant for people," Tarte added.

"If I ever end up having to fight the hero, even this wouldn't be enough to kill her. I'd like to use Gungnir, but that's not reliable in a fight. I came up with this as another option."

My quest for a powerful spell that was still usable in combat had led me to Cannon Volley.

"This is going too far!" Dia insisted.

"Like I said, even this isn't strong enough... I fought her, so I know," I explained.

The hero was stupidly powerful.

"All right, I'm done with testing my new killing move. Let's move on to practice. We haven't had a wide field like this to use in a long time. Show me the fruits of your labors."

"Sounds good. I'll show you how much I've grown," declared Dia.

"I'm still getting stronger, too!" Tarte asserted.

I gave them both a thorough training session. Perhaps because of the good food and open space, the workout seemed to go better than usual. By the end, Dia was so exhausted, I had to carry her back to the academy.

"Lord Lugh, today was a lot of fun," Tarte said.

"Yeah, it was. Spending time outside is fun," I replied.

The day had made for a good break from the normal.

I have to check on my trap when I get back. Catching that assassin was the one thing that could make the day better.

I slipped out of my apartment in the middle of the night. I was going to check on the status of the ploy I'd set.

Ever since I'd heard from my dad that there was an assassin going after Epona, I'd been staying near her as much as possible to observe her surroundings. While doing so, I'd managed to detect the hired killer's presence a few times.

They were cautious and decently skilled, however. Not once had they presented me with a chance to catch them.

So I'd changed my strategy. If I couldn't apprehend the assassin, I would instead draw them out. The plan was to fabricate a situation that convinced them to act.

To create that scenario, I'd been behaving like I was Epona's secret guard. However, I moved in a way that would betray that supposed identity to those skilled enough.

Humans were strange in that they had a tendency not to believe the information they heard from other people, but then unconditionally accept anything they discovered themselves. My current plan seized upon the advantage of that phenomenon. I wanted the assassin to notice me and think of me as the hero's bodyguard. If they did, they'd undoubtedly try to go after Epona when I wasn't around.

I made sure the killer knew I was absent today by having Naoise watch Epona in my place. Leaving Epona completely unprotected risked arousing suspicion on whether I actually was defending her.

Naoise, however, as skilled a sword fighter as he was, knew nothing of the methods of assassins and had no experience safeguarding another. Naoise would definitely give the killer a chance to strike, and I trusted they would have the skill to take advantage.

With me out of the picture, the assassin had no reason not to strike, provided they could get past Naoise.

I snuck into Epona's room from above the ceiling. There were only so many advantageous positions from which to kill covertly, and this was the one I'd picked. If the enemy was going to try for Epona's life, they were already hiding in a similar location.

...*I've got them.* They were nearby. My intention that night wasn't to stop a murder but to successfully mark the would-be killer.

They must have infiltrated the apartment only to withdraw after deciding they couldn't get the job done with their current equipment. Epona does look helpless, though.

Epona was sound asleep. Even though I, an assassin, was just a few feet away. She wasn't remotely aware of my presence. A Cannon Strike at this distance wouldn't leave so much as a scratch on her, however. Even Cannon Volley wasn't enough to end the hero.

All right, time to go. My trap was successful.

...Tomorrow I should be able to pinpoint the assassin.

◇

The next morning, I left for the academy as usual. Using my Tuatha Dé eyes, I observed everyone I walked past on the way to class to search for the mark I had placed on the assassin yesterday.

It was highly likely that the killer was a member of the faculty.

The security at school was tight. Infiltrating it from the outside was extremely difficult. That much went without saying, though. Every noble family in Alvan had a child at the academy.

"Lord Lugh, you've been looking around restlessly today. Is something wrong?" Tarte asked.

"Wow, you noticed that?"

I was surprised. As Tarte said, I was eyeing my surroundings. I didn't think I was doing anything that betrayed my motives, however. I was employing the full scope of my vision without looking at anything directly. To other people, I should've appeared as I always had.

"I just had a feeling. Your mood felt a little different," Tarte stated.

"I see. You're a smart girl."

I patted Tarte on the head, and her eyes narrowed happily.

As an assassin, there was nothing more important than being highly aware of your environs. Failing to pick up on small signals could mean death.

"Hey, how come Tarte gets all the praise? Guess I need to try harder," Dia grumbled.

"I just commended you yesterday for that spell, right?" I reminded.

"That's entirely different." Dia puffed out her cheeks. It was adorable when she got competitive.

Thankfully, it didn't seem as though the assassin was in my class. That came as a relief. I didn't want to have to kill a classmate I'd formed a bond with.

After class, I made an excuse to go to Professor Dune's office. He was clean, too.

For lunch, Dia, Tarte, and I went to the dining hall instead of the courtyard like we usually did. It afforded me a much better opportunity to observe students. Tarte and Dia remained oblivious to my motive and merely enjoyed the food.

"This is so good... I'm surprised," said Tarte.

"It's really expensive, though," added Dia.

"That's because they use good ingredients," I commented.

Our meals really were delicious. Tarte's cooking usually kept me away from the dining hall, but I didn't think sampling the academy's luxurious cuisine once in a while was all that bad. The quality of the dishes couldn't be denied. Dia was correct when she'd said they were expensive, however. Unlike with breakfast and dinner, you had to pay for lunch out of your pocket. The cost was pretty high for a lowly baron's son.

"It's more than just good ingredients. The preparation is excellent, too. The chicken in this stew is incredible—its flavor has dissolved into the broth, but it's still juicy and delicious. It's like magic," Tarte observed keenly.

She was so fired up about the cooking that she looked ready to rush into the kitchen and ask for the recipe. Ambition really was one of Tarte's best traits.

While admiring Tarte, I looked around the dining hall.

There you are.

The trap I'd placed was a special kind of powder coating. I'd left a bit of the stuff in every conceivable place an assassin might've entered Epona's room from.

The dust was a gray-white substance that was nearly microscopic. A person couldn't notice it sticking to them. Water wouldn't wash it away, either. To my Tuatha Dé eyes, it glowed a bright blue.

"Wow, it's him."

The assassin was a marquis's son who'd only just barely made it into Class A.

I felt a sense of undeniable appreciation for my opponent.

I'd known this guy to be skilled. With his ability, he could've made it into Class S. Like a true professional, however, he intentionally entered at a lower rank so he wouldn't stand out. He was even wise enough to choose Class A so that he'd have a room to himself and maintain his distance from others.

I had intentionally entered Class S to be as close to Epona as possible to search for her weak points, but trying to keep your distance and not stand out was the more straightforward and more common approach for a hired killer.

However, the fact that he took my bait so readily demonstrated a lack of self-restraint.

"Oh no, it looks like Lord Lugh is enjoying the dining hall food, too. But I won't lose! I'll make something even better than this!"

Tarte mistakenly took my relaxed facial expression to mean I was enjoying my meal.

"Lugh, I think we can count on a special dinner tonight," Dia quipped.

"Yeah, she's got that look in her eyes," I replied.

Dia and I both looked at Tarte and smiled.

Since Tarte was going to put a lot of effort into our dinner, I decided to take care of my job afterward.

Once classes had finished, I met with the headmaster and a few others. The academy was going to be losing a student, so specific preparations needed to be made.

After much discussion, we decided the cover story would be that the target couldn't take the school's strict lifestyle and ran off. Evidence of his escape had already been fabricated, including cutting part of the fence.

The headmaster would tell the guards to provide eyewitness testimony of the assassin's flight. As an extra precaution, some fabric was to be placed on the fence to make it look like the boy's uniform tore as he was running. The hero was paramount, so the academy spared no expense.

Later that night, I donned a disguise and snuck into the Class A dorm. It didn't take any clever maneuvers. I simply walked through the front door while everyone was sleeping and headed straight for the assassin's room. It was late enough that no one was outside their rooms and the lights were all out.

Silent as a ghost, I used the key the headmaster had given me to enter the assassin's room.

I checked to see that my target was sleeping and then threw a knife. I used my Tuatha Dé eyes to observe his mana capacity and adjusted the attack accordingly.

The knife pierced his comforter and plunged deep into his body. Blood spread from the wound, but the young man didn't even scream.

That was because the edge of my weapon had been coated with a neurotoxin that took immediate effect. It rendered one unable even to lift a finger once it entered the body. Not only did this keep a victim from screaming, it also prevented suicide.

There was bewilderment on the assassin's face as he looked at me. He probably hadn't expected Epona's guard to make such a direct move.

He wasn't good enough. He lacked the wariness required of his profession.

"Sorry about this. I can't let you get in the way of my job. It's meaningless at this point, but I'm going to give you a piece of advice. As an assassin, you always have to assume you are being hunted... Though to be fair, I have made the same mistake before."

I knocked him unconscious, stopped his bleeding, stuffed him and his bloodied sheets into a bag, and slung him over my shoulder.

Just as when I'd entered the dormitory, I simply walked down the empty hallways. I'd memorized the guard's route and timing, so there was no risk of being spotted.

My methods had been straightforward this time, and less complicated procedures meant a higher success rate. An assassination should only be as intricate as the situation demanded.

...*Now that this is done, I can carry him to my hideout.*

I'd prepared a secret location in preparation for this sort of thing. It was a place where I could make as much noise as I wanted without attracting any attention. I needed to get my captive to give me his employer's name and the motive for wanting Epona dead.

His usefulness didn't end there, of course. I'd finally gotten hold of a mage. I planned to use him as practice for the surgical implantation of Tuatha Dé eyes. Tarte wanted the surgery, and I needed to be confident I could do it safely.

This is going to be a busy night. It might be tough to stay awake in class tomorrow.

We were taking a written exam in class today. Once I finished all the problems, I fell deep into thought.

It had been a few days since I assassinated the assassin.

…I didn't get much information out of him. Through torture, I learned the mastermind was a member of the noble faction. I'd reported that finding to both my dad and the headmaster.

It was a huge relief it wasn't a royal who'd put the hit out on the hero. House Tuatha Dé was part of the royal faction, and we couldn't afford any internal conflicts. If you looked at the big picture, though, the very existence of such cells spoke to infighting.

I had also learned why they were going after Epona. In a sense, it was a very respectable reason.

Anyway, it's finally time.

I was off to perform Tarte's surgery tonight. I'd had enough practice, and we conveniently had a few days of vacation beginning the following day.

Tarte was going to have to wear eyepatches for a couple of days, so conducting the procedure on the night before a stint of vacation was the best time.

"Your time is up. I'm now going to collect your answer sheets."

Professor Dune collected our exams. Shortly afterward, the bell rang, announcing the end of the lesson.

Dia and Tarte rushed over to me, followed by one more person who'd made a habit of following us around lately.

"Lugh, I did really well on the test this time. It was all thanks to our study group," Epona said.

She'd entered this class significantly behind everyone else from a learning standpoint, so I'd had many opportunities to teach her how to study. We were meeting for study sessions frequently, but because trying to work out our schedule every time we met was time-consuming, we'd decided to establish a regular time to meet as a group.

Even Naoise and Finn had joined our meetings.

"You've got the basics down. If you keep going at this pace, half a year from now, you won't need our help at all," I praised.

"I'm gonna keep working hard. I can't let myself fall behind," Epona declared.

"That's the spirit," I said.

This is getting scary. Just how quickly is she going to grow?

Epona made a face like she wanted to say something, so I urged her to spit it out.

"Why are you going this far for me?" she asked. "Is it because I'm the hero?" Her gaze was cast down at the floor.

Epona was poor with interpersonal relationships. Even though she depended on me, her lack of confidence made her feel unworthy. In turn, that caused her to grow distrustful.

"If I said that didn't have anything to do with it, I'd be lying. But I swear that's not the only reason. I help because I enjoy spending time with you. I'm a bad liar. I get in a terrible mood when I'm around people I don't like."

"Okay, that's good to hear. I was worried you didn't like doing things with me… Someday I'll repay you for all you've done for me!" Epona promised.

I'd told similar falsehoods many times before, but such deception was necessary. Everything I did was to find Epona's weak points. I had to work toward a future where I didn't have to end her life.

"We need to get to the library, or they'll cancel our reserved seats," Tarte said, antsy about the time.

"Ah, you're right. The library is very unforgiving. If you're late by even a second, they'll give your chair to someone else," Dia affirmed.

"That's true," I replied. "But if the library doesn't work, we can always just go to our apartment. We have plenty of space in there."

""NO.""

Tarte and Dia shot my suggestion down in unison.

What's wrong with using our apartment? Tarte kept the place very clean. There was nothing damning Epona could find, either. My work's nature meant I owned things the hero shouldn't see, but they were all well hidden.

"Ha-ha-ha, you're completely under their thumbs, Lugh. But living under the iron grip of Dia and Tarte sounds quite pleasant. How about lending one of them to me?" Naoise joked.

"In your dreams. They're both important partners to me," I shot back.

After that declaration, Dia and Tarte's faces flushed, and Epona muttered, "That's so nice," with a look like a child lusting after a toy.

"Anyway, let's get going. We are truly going to be late if we don't leave now," I urged. Gathering my things, I stood to leave.

It was now the evening of our first day of vacation. I was facing Tarte, who had a bandage over one of her eyes.

Last night, I'd completed the safe implantation of a Tuatha Dé eye. In a few moments, we would know the result of my efforts.

"I'm nervous. I hope Tarte is still able to see out of that eye," Dia admitted.

"She responded well enough to the surgery, but there is still a minimal chance it could've failed. I'm anxious, too," I replied.

That other assassin had made for good practice. I'd only agreed to work on Tarte because I'd been entirely sure of myself.

"Ah, Lord Lugh, Lady Dia, it's almost time." Tarte pressed her hand against the patch over her right eye.

"I'm going to take the bandage off, but I want to say something first. Don't worry about my feelings. I know you'll be tempted to lie and say you can see even if you can't," I said.

"…You're right…," Tarte conceded.

That was just the sort of person Tarte was.

"At least promise me you won't do that. If something feels off, I'll be able to do something about it if you tell me early on. The longer you keep it from me, the more difficult it will be to correct any errors. Don't worry about how trivial it might feel. If there's anything that feels strange, tell me, okay?"

"Okay, I swear," answered Tarte.

Tarte's uncovered left eye shone brightly at me. I could see my reflection in it. Gently, I removed the bandages around her right eye.

The surgery had left her iris looking slightly darker. When Tuatha Dé underwent the procedure, their eyes turned gray. In Tarte's case, however, the pigmentation simply dropped a bit.

Her right eye was out of focus because it'd been covered for so long.

"Everything looks so blurred, my lord."

"That's because your eye was bound for an entire day. Look into this."

Using mana, I conjured up a little light. As Tarte stared into it, her eye began to focus.

"I can see properly now," she said after a minute or two.

"Okay, moving on. Come over here."

I took Tarte by the hand and led her to the window. After opening it, I pointed to a distant mountain.

"First, look at that mountain with your left eye," I instructed.

"I can see it clearly," Tarte answered.

"Good. Now, look at the large tree at the summit. How many branches are there extending from the trunk? Can you tell me what kinds of animals are on those branches?"

"I can't see that. I can't even see the tree."

You would've needed binoculars to spot something that far away.

"Okay. Try doing the same with your right eye."

"Wow, there really is a big tree. I can even tell how many branches there are. It's faint, but I can't believe I can see something that far away. There are sixteen branches. Sixteen! But the small animals on the branches are blurry, and I can't tell what they are."

"Try pouring mana into your eyes with physical strengthening. Be careful not to do it too quickly. Take it nice and slow."

"Ah, I can see more now. There's a squirrel, and also three birds I've never seen before, and hmm...there's a longhorn beetle, too."

Tarte could see a bug sitting on a branch that was kilometers away. Such was the power of Tuatha Dé eyes.

"That's more than enough. Can you see anything else?" I asked.

"After strengthening my eye with mana, it now looks like there are glittering beads of light around you, Lady Dia, and around myself," Tarte replied.

"What you're seeing is mana. Try strengthening your eye a little more. If you do that, you'll be able to see the mana that inhabits the world."

"Ah, it's beautiful. This must be the mana in the atmosphere—the power of the world. Wooow, it's so pretty. Who knew everything was this beautiful? This is the way my lord sees things!"

With an ecstatic expression on her face, Tarte spun around, her skirt waving in the air.

"There's no problem with your long-distance vision and your ability to see mana. Now for the real test. I'm going to check to test your ability to see objects in motion. Tarte, get as close to the wall as you can," I commanded.

"Like this?"

"Perfect. I'm going to throw a ball, and I want you to catch it. Please pour even more mana into your eye. Make it much stronger."

I took out one of my assassination tools. It looked like an unremarkable, white, fist-sized sphere. After scribbling something on the little orb, I held it up in the air.

I strengthened myself with mana. Tarte was able to see that, so she did the same thing and poured even more mana into her eye.

After confirming her physical strengthening, I raised the ball overhead and threw it. Because I'd empowered myself with mana, it rocketed from my fingers at over two hundred forty kilometers per hour.

Unsurprisingly, Tarte caught it.

Catching an object that was traveling so quickly was undoubtedly an impressive feat, but Tarte could do that even before the surgery. What I wanted to confirm was something else.

"Wow, we're going to celebrate?! I'm so happy."

"Good, you passed. You now have what I've always wanted to give you: an eye that can see at high speeds."

"Huh? Lugh, Tarte, what do you mean by 'celebrate'? No one said anything about that!" said Dia, her eyes darting back and forth between us.

"I wrote a message on the ball," I explained.

"The words were plain as day to me, even though they were spinning," Tarte added.

"Those Tuatha Dé eyes are amazing. I couldn't see that at all," Dia admitted.

It came as no surprise that Dia couldn't read the ball. Not only had it been moving at over two hundred forty kilometers an hour, but it had also been rotating more than one hundred times a second. Reading a message on something in such a state was impossible for normal eyes.

"We should go to the royal capital. Things are expensive there, but it should be fine so long as we don't visit too often," I said.

The royal capital was a two-hour carriage ride from the academy. Prices were extremely high, but the city was rife with the highest-quality goods you could imagine, and there was no better place to experience luxury.

"Yeah, you're right. We'll make it a celebration for Tarte's successful surgery. We should enjoy ourselves!" Dia exclaimed.

"I'm looking forward to this chance to study lots of different foods," Tarte commented.

It would've been nice if Tarte could just forget about everything and have some simple fun for once, but I did like her earnest side.

"Lord Lugh, the successful procedure on my right eye means you'll do surgery on my left eye, too, right?" asked Tarte.

"Yeah, but to be careful, we're going to wait a few days. We're back in school tomorrow anyway. We should do it the night before our next break. In the meantime, I want you to wear this." I handed Tarte something I'd been keeping for this moment.

"It's so small and clear. What is it?" she inquired.

"It's a contact lens. If you wear that on your left eye, it will appear the same color as your right one. Everyone would be surprised if one of your eyes suddenly changed color," I explained.

"Oh, that's right. I'll make sure to wear it," Tarte agreed.

"Tomorrow's training will probably be tough, but try your best to push through it. Once you get used to your new eyes, you'll grow leagues stronger than you ever could've before," I stated.

"Then I'll be able to support you better than ever!" Tarte cheerily concluded.

"You'll also be able to make better use of the wind magic I've made for you… I need some kind of secret weapon of my own. You two are going to leave me in the dust," Dia observed.

I'd only just removed Tarte's eye wrappings, so I had to take it easy on her today. Come tomorrow, however, I planned to subject her to combat training that would force her to adapt to her Tuatha Dé eye. All that extra sensory information was going to put a burden on her brain. Time and practice were required for her to get used to it.

"Don't worry about trying not to spend too much money at the capital. I've prepared a special budget for this trip," I said.

"Ooooh, then let's get some really expensive alcohol," Dia suggested excitedly.

"I'll order some beef from a cow that was raised specifically for eating. I've heard rumors about such cattle, and I've wanted to try some at least once in my lifetime. I heard that meat from those cows is significantly softer and tastier than from those that do field work," Tarte added.

They both knew that holding back when I'd asked them not to would come off as rude. It sounded like we were in for a fun day out.

I had to ensure we hadn't been tailed. A lowly baron's son indulging himself at high-class restaurants in the royal capital could start some unsavory rumors. I decided to take the girls to a nice eatery that offered isolated rooms to protect the customers' privacy.

"Let's all get changed before we leave. We're going somewhere fancy, so we need to look the part," I said.

"I'll wear the dress you bought me in Milteu, my lord," Tarte replied.

"Oh yeah, I have a dress that will captivate you, Lugh," Dia answered.

I'm looking forward to seeing their dresses. I suppose I should change as well.

Our classes had ended early today. It seemed to me like everyone was having a hard time paying attention during lessons. Once every two months, a special event was held to help the students refuel. One of them was happening now.

I called out to Epona, who was looking noticeably unsure of what to do with herself.

"Have you decided what you're going to buy today?" I inquired.

"I have no idea. I don't know too much about the names of the stores and stuff like that. But I am really looking forward to going shopping. My hero's salary is paying me well."

Epona held up a leather coin pouch.

"It sounds like the Academy Market is going to be very lively. I'm sure you'll find something that catches your eye," I assured.

The Academy Market was the event meant to help students relax.

Our school was just north of the royal capital, which was the only option students had for recreation away from the academy. The trouble was that the city was expensive, no matter what you did. Only those chosen could live there, and the stores were tailored to the wealthiest of clientele.

That wasn't an issue for those on the aristocracy's upper end, but lesser nobles weren't really capable of enjoying the capital to its fullest.

The Academy Market had been established to deal with that. The school reached out to various popular companies around the country and invited them to run market stalls on academy grounds for three days. Goods were set at the same prices as the main stores, so even less wealthy students could have a good time without worrying about travel costs. Many participating companies even provided limited items and debuted brand new products.

A lot of my peers could hardly contain their excitement, knowing that popular stores from throughout the Alvanian Kingdom and even some international vendors were going to attend.

"Is there anything you two want, Dia and Tarte?" I questioned.

"Nothing comes to mind for me, so I think I'm going to walk around first and see if anything catches my eye," answered Tarte.

"Hmm, there's nothing I want, so I'm going to head back to the dorm," replied Dia.

That seemed like uncharacteristic behavior for Dia. She had always been the curious type. I would've thought she would be chomping at the bit for an opportunity like this.

As I pondered it further, I realized she'd been restless the past few days. Something was definitely off. I'd caught a glance of her counting her money this morning. It seemed likely that she already knew what she wanted to buy and didn't want to tell us what it was.

I'm curious about whatever Dia is hiding, but I'll leave it be for now.

"You all look like you're having a fun little chat. Mind if I join in?" A blond young man was approaching us.

"Hey, Naoise. We're talking about what we're going to

purchase at the Academy Market. I'm sure you don't have any interest in this event," I remarked.

He was a son of one of the four major dukedoms. He could afford to buy as much as he wanted, even in the royal capital. I'd also learned he regularly invited people to the royal capital to sway them into joining the little group he'd been building.

"What are you saying? I love the Academy Market. There are things money alone can't buy. For example, the main attraction this time is a company called Natural You. Rumor is they're going to unveil a new product here today. As a fan, I can't overlook this opportunity," explained Naoise.

"...You're interested in Natural You?" I asked, somewhat surprised.

"Women aren't the only people who use makeup. Their moisturizer has been a big help to me."

It's indeed best for men to moisturize as well, but I hadn't been expecting him to say that.

As Naoise had said, the cosmetics brand I'd founded as Illig Balor, Natural You, was also running a stall during the school event. I was planning on heading over there later to pick up the report for the follow-up investigation I'd requested of Maha.

"Ah, it's starting," said Tarte. The announcement that the market was opening echoed throughout the school.

Everyone rushed as fast as possible to the plaza.

The Academy Market was available only to students on its first day. It would be open to the public on its remaining two days. That was why all the students were hurrying to buy things today. Once the event was available to outside customers, it would only get more challenging to find what you wanted.

"We should get moving, or all the good items will be gone," I urged.

"Okay! Um, are you really okay not going, Lady Dia?" Tarte pressed.

"Yeah, I'm fine. Don't worry about me," Dia answered.

"Let's go, Tarte. We'll bring home a present for you, Dia," I said.

Dia didn't want us around for her secret shopping. It seemed okay to let her do what she wanted this time.

Tarte and I dove into the swaths of teenagers.

Despite only having just begun, the Academy Market was in full swing.

"There are so many people here," Tarte observed.

"Just about the entire school is attending," I replied.

About two hundred students were at our school, but all the live-in faculty brought that number even higher. Because the academy also functioned as a stronghold, there were personnel here for that purpose as well.

Tarte opened a map that detailed the location of each shop's stand. Every student had been given one before the event had begun. The pamphlet also provided simple descriptions for each participating company.

"There are so many famous stores. I don't know where to begin. Why are all these famous stores going through the trouble of coming all the way here anyway?" asked Tarte.

"Good question. They won't be making a profit from this. The academy allows them to set up the stands only on the condition that they set the prices at the same level as their main retail stores, after all... What these businesses are banking on is turning us into lasting customers and spreading word of mouth. Most of the students here are from noble families. Promoting to students is a good way to gain long-term customers," I explained.

The cost of transport alone surely meant many businesses were taking a loss. In the eyes of a shrewd entrepreneur, however, that lost money was like paying for advertising.

Many companies undoubtedly had high hopes for those visitors who would arrive tomorrow and the next day, too. It was tough to gain permission to open a store in the royal capital, so any opportunity to sell to the city's customers was valuable.

"That didn't occur to me at all. Business is really complicated," Tarte stated.

"It is. It's a difficult world," I responded.

"Ohhh, it sounds way too hard for me."

To become a top-rate businessperson, you needed more than just work ethic. Mercantile acumen was also required. Without such things, you were doomed before you ever began. A proper eye for enterprise counted for a lot.

"Um, are you sure it's okay for me to come with you two?" Epona asked.

"Of course. I don't mind. You're a classmate, and this will be more fun with company," I assured.

"Yeah! This is the first time I've ever gone shopping with people like this," Tarte added.

Together, the three of us made our way around the area and perused the stalls. There were tons of exciting products, but that was to be expected of such popular retailers.

If you were attentive, you could spot staff from all the stores peeking into rival stalls. In a way, that was another merit of the Academy Market—popular stores could learn from one another.

While stuffing ourselves with rare steamed sweets wrapped in transparent dough, Tarte, Epona, and I walked around to each stall, buying anything that interested us. Even just strolling around was enjoyable.

Tarte's eyes lit up when we passed a particular stand. "Wow. This cloth is so beautiful, and such a light shade of pink. I wonder how they managed to dye it this color. This one is sky-blue!" she exclaimed.

"This color is Mireille's...," Epona muttered.

Tarte had stopped at a clothing store's booth. It also sold raw materials.

"Yeah, you don't see bright colors like this very often," I remarked.

The fabrics were dyed pink and sky-blue. The vibrant colors themselves were the store's flagship product. Their material was high quality, but producing textiles in such vivid colors was the bigger draw.

I recalled that the pink and blue dyes were specialty products only produced in an impoverished region of Alvan. After the pigments caught this company's attention, they negotiated a contract that gave them exclusive use of the colorants, allowing the business to sell them on a large scale.

"This cloth is so lovely, and cheap, too! I know Lady Esri would be happy to get some as a gift," Tarte commented.

My mom enjoyed making new outfits. Tarte was right in thinking she'd want such high-quality material.

"I'm taking care of the souvenirs, so you don't have to worry about that. You just focus on what you want to buy," I reminded.

"But she's done so much for me," protested Tarte.

"I actually want to get something for her, too. So yeah, you can pick it out, and I'll pay for it. Let's make it a present from the two of us," I stated.

"O-okay. Thanks…"

"Don't worry about it. Right now, you have a better idea of my mother's tastes than I do. I have no choice but to leave it to you. At least let me pay for it," I said.

"Okay, I understand!"

Tarte began to inspect the different fabrics with a severe expression on her face. She was taking this too seriously.

This could take a while…

I looked over at Epona. Curiously, she was staring at some of the items on display with a wistful look in her eyes.

If she'd told me she was a girl, I could've bought her something as a present, but as far as she knew, I still thought her to be a boy. Giving a supposed male student female clothing would've made me look like a pervert.

"I picked one, my lord. I'm going to get this strange light-pink color."

Tarte's voice brought me out of my contemplation. In her hands was a bolt of pink fabric. This color reminded me of the cherry blossom trees from my home in my previous life. Perhaps Tarte found the shade unusual because she'd never seen cherry blossoms.

"The texture feels nice, and I think my mother will like this shade. I'm sure it'd look good on you, too, Tarte," I observed.

"That doesn't have anything to do with it," she replied.

"I'd say it does. You're the one who wears the clothes my mother makes, after all," I reminded.

"Th-that is true."

My mother enjoyed treating Tarte like her own personal dress-up doll.

"Epona."

I called out to the hero, but she didn't respond. Her gaze was transfixed on a sky-blue dress. It seemed like unusual behavior, even for the flighty young woman.

"Epona!"

"Y-yes?"

"We're going to go look at other stalls, but if there's something you want to buy here, then we can split up."

"Okay, let's do that. Sorry."

"No, it's fine."

Epona had been raised as a boy. Perhaps that was why she'd found girl clothing so captivating. If that was the case, I decided it was better that Tarte and I weren't around. The hero wouldn't be able to buy an outfit meant for a girl if people who were supposed to think she was male were around.

After three hours, Tarte and I had finished making our rounds at the Academy Market.

"We ended up with a lot of stuff," I said.

"I might have gone a little overboard. But that was really satisfying," Tarte replied, carrying around a bag and looking pleased with herself. Tarte was decently wealthy. My family had been paying her a retainer's salary ever since she'd arrived in Tuatha Dé, and she hadn't had much in the way of living expenses.

"Sorry, Tarte, but do you mind heading back without me?" I asked.

"You're meeting with Maha, right?"

"No, I'm just going to pick up the results of an investigation. Maha is busy, so I doubt she came all the way out here."

A round trip from Milteu took multiple days. As the Natural You brand's proxy representative, Maha was very busy, and her time was valuable.

"No, she's definitely here. There's no way Maha would pass up a chance to see you, my lord!" stated Tarte confidently.

I won't mind if she's right.

"If she *is* here, then would you want to come, too?" I questioned.

"No, I'll go back. Maha undoubtedly wants it to be just the two of you. I can be with you all the time, but the same can't be said for her. I'd feel bad if I didn't give her some alone time with you."

"That's what she wants?"

"That's what she wants."

Tarte and Maha were close, so I would've thought Maha wanted to see her, too, but if Tarte said otherwise, then that probably wasn't the case.

Tarte and I went our separate ways, and I headed for the Natural You stall.

Despite it only being the first day of the event, there was already a line that wound outward from my company's stand. The market wasn't open to the public yet, and there were already so many people. I could only guess at what things would be like tomorrow. It was a good reminder of how popular Natural You was.

All right, what should I do? My plan had been to be taken to the back of the stall after providing an excuse about wanting to test some products. This long line was going to make that difficult, however.

I thought I felt a familiar presence behind me, and then someone put an arm around one of mine.

"Hey, handsome, would you like to go on a date with me?" invited a young woman who glanced up at me amorously.

Her sleek, blue hair was concealed under a hat today, and she'd used makeup to disguise herself slightly. Instead of her usual attire, she was wearing something sweet and stylish.

Even with such differences, there was no way I wouldn't recognize the girl. She wasn't just a friend; she was family.

"That sounds great. There's a nice pop-up café nearby. Want to go there and get some sweets?" I proposed.

"That would be lovely. Shall we be off?"

"Okay."

The young girl—Maha—beamed.

Tarte had read the situation correctly. It looked like Maha had gone to a lot of trouble just to come here and spend time with me.

It was surprising to see her in disguise, but that served a practical purpose. As the face of Natural You, Maha had become something of a celebrity. She counted many nobles among her acquaintances. If anyone recognized her, it would probably cause a commotion.

We entered the café together. Thankfully, it wasn't too crowded when we stopped by.

The place was famous for its high-quality herbal tea and unique desserts. I'd actually been interested in the company that ran the little restaurant because they were supposedly prevalent in an eastern city. The pop-up café they'd set up used academy facilities, which afforded secluded rooms perfect for private conversations.

"...Maha, are we really ordering this?" I asked.

"Yes, we're pretending to be a couple, so we don't raise any suspicion. We have to order something that makes us look the part," Maha replied with a spirited grin.

We both ordered the signature herbal tea, as well as one extra-large parfait. It was called the Super Lovey Dovey Parfait, so asking for it understandably took some courage.

Our tea arrived first.

"This smells so good," Maha remarked.

"Yeah, it's relaxing. I see why this restaurant is so popular," I added.

"...But Natural You's tea is better. If this restaurant is doing so well, we should be able to do better. Maybe we shouldn't just sell tea leaves, but also open a café business?" Maha proposed.

The tea Maha was talking about was made from tea leaves imported using a trade route that Maha herself had pioneered. I'd devised a way to brew them using techniques from my previous life. My method resulted in a more potent fragrance and crisper taste than the local style.

Natural You had been seeking out high-quality tea leaves because they appealed to our target audience of wealthy women. I had high hopes that expanding into beverages would land us another hit product.

"Opening up a café would be interesting. But we'd need help. Operating any sort of restaurant requires an entirely different business model than what we've been operating under. We might have to fumble in the dark a bit until we figure out what we're doing. I'm not sure there's anyone we can entrust such work to," I explained.

"Yes there is, dear brother. Since you returned to Tuatha Dé, I've been training some promising children. They'd be perfect for the café," Maha explained.

"Oh, you think those kids are up to it?" I asked.

"Yes... I owe you my thanks, dear brother. You told me not to keep my personal feelings out of business operations and encouraged me to follow my heart. It was your words that emboldened me to bring them on. It may have been motivated by my self-interest, but I'm sure the company will benefit nonetheless."

The children Maha was referring to were the orphans she did business with back when she'd been living on the streets. They'd been snatched up and separated by different orphanages hoping to collect government subsidies, but Maha had worked on getting them back together. She was confident they'd be a marvelous boon to my corporation.

After adopting the kids, Maha trained them by having them work at a series of stores owned by the Balor Company.

I was doubtful of her plan, but all the branches that had taken Maha's old friends in spoke highly of them. Many shops had been hesitant to let the children leave because of their excellent performance. Some even went as far as to say they'd pay a fee to keep them on permanently.

Like Maha, the orphans had learned to use their wits to survive and run a business despite the massive handicap of being young orphans. They were persistent, learned quickly, and were always rife with ideas.

Maha's friends had turned out to be a treasure trove of talented employees for Natural You. Businesses weren't usually able to gather such a plentiful supply of competent personnel. Maha had done a splendid job of accomplishing her personal goal of saving her old friends and ensuring Natural You's success.

"I said that because I trust you, Maha. There's no reason to thank me," I said.

"Hearing you say that makes me want to work even harder. Just you watch. Natural You still has room to grow," she replied.

Maha really was dependable. With her around, I didn't have to worry about my enterprises, and I could live my life as Lugh Tuatha Dé.

The parfait finally arrived. It was a super-sized parfait made to be eaten by a couple. The Super Lovey Dovey Parfait was a monstrosity with a cringeworthy name.

"…This is way too much for two people to eat," I observed.

"Don't worry. I'm a big fan of sweets," Maha replied.

The mountainous dessert had been amassed in a giant mug rather than a regular-sized cup. The flagon was made out of clear, valuable glass.

Sponge cake, strawberry jelly, sponge cake, strawberry cream, sponge cake, and strawberry jam. The parfait was made up of layers of sponge cake with various sweets in between, and on top there was a large serving of whipped cream and sliced strawberries. There were red, heart-shaped sugar candies buried throughout.

...Just looking at it is giving me heartburn.

Two spoons had been stuck into the mug as well. Each one was absurdly long.

"It'll be tough to eat with such long utensils. What were they thinking with these?" I said.

"The reason the spoons are like that is so you can do this."

With a smile on her face, Maha scooped up a spoonful of cream and then held her spoon in front of my mouth.

"I see. The length is so you can feed your partner. This parfait really is made for couples."

"That's right. Can you hurry up and eat that for me? I want to eat, too." Maha shook her spoon in front of my face.

"This is pretty embarrassing, though," I admitted.

"...You're too cruel. You don't know how many all-nighters I pulled to be able to come here, and you won't even indulge me with this one thing," pouted Maha.

She started to blatantly fake cry. Fake tears aside, I couldn't deny that she'd worked very hard to see me.

Thank goodness this is a private room. If these had been open seats, I would've been way too embarrassed to do this.

I took Maha's spoon in my mouth. The whipped cream was very light. It was airy and moderately sweet, yet it possessed a robust flavor.

After realizing how good the parfait tasted, it suddenly didn't seem impossible to finish.

"You're up next, dear brother."

"I have to feed you, too?"

"...I went to such painstaking lengths to gather all the information you requested. Surely that's enough to earn this small act of kindness?"

Maha traced her lips with a finger. It was quite a suggestive gesture.

I smiled wryly, scooped up some of the pile of sweets with my spoon, and held it to Maha's lips. She happily ate it, savoring the taste in her mouth.

...This is even more embarrassing than I thought it would be.

"It's so good. I'm confident in our tea, but we won't be able to succeed if I don't do some thorough research into dessert," Maha said.

"I'm impressed you're able to think about business under these circumstances. The embarrassment is driving me crazy," I responded.

"This isn't easy for me, either. That's precisely why I'm trying to hide my embarrassment. Okay, next is the strawberry jam and sponge cake layer. Let's keep going. Uncovering new flavors as we eat is exciting. Despite it being so large, the different tastes as you work your way down really keep you eating. This is some valuable information," observed Maha.

After I fed Maha, it was now her turn to spoon me some.

This is still embarrassing, but I need to push through it.

We continued to feed each other.

It took us thirty minutes, but we somehow succeeded in taking down a noticeable portion of the parfait.

I'm tired. Mentally and physically.

"That was so much food," I said, exhausted.

"Yeah. We only barely got through it... The item must have an impact, but when I serve this kind of dessert at my restaurant, I think I'll reduce the size a bit," noted Maha.

Maha looked pretty uncomfortable. She wasn't usually the type to eat very much.

"...Okay, I've gotten my reward. Let's move on to work."

"Yes, that would be a big help. I'm ready."

I used a spell to probe the area and make sure no one was spying on us. At the same time, I created a cage of wind to prevent sound from leaking out of our room. We could now talk about confidential matters without any risk.

"First, let's go over what I learned about Epona Rhiannon. It wasn't easy, but I obtained interesting information from the Royal Order... She is stuck between a promise and a traumatic event. That might be her biggest weakness."

Maha handed me a folder of papers, and I quickly leafed through them. Contained therein were many theories regarding the hero, along with evidence to support them.

From the way Epona had acted during the mock battle, I'd thought she was a fighting enthusiast, but I was wrong. It was more complicated than that. An obsession had wormed its way into her mind.

"I'm impressed you were able to gather this much information," I praised.

"You did tell me to be scrupulous," replied Maha.

She made it sound simple, but this was no ordinary report. It was detailed information that could ruin Epona if it ever got out.

"This information will be the key to reaching her heart," Maha stated.

"With your report and what I know about Epona's personality, I'm sure she's over there right now," I said.

"I agree. You should get going, dear brother."

Maha had handed me additional documents containing information on a traumatic event in Epona's history and the person at the center of it. This information was the ultimate weapon in my fight to get Epona to open up to me.

Reading over Maha's intel also made me realize another misconception of mine. At the clothing stall, Epona hadn't been staring at a dress because she'd never had a chance to dress like a girl. She'd been reminiscing.

That's when I remembered that the vivid dyes the clothing company had grown rich off of were the special product of a certain rural domain in the Alvanian Kingdom. And that region was...

"You don't mind if I leave?" I checked.

"Not at all. You've treated me to a nice date. I'm satisfied... No, that's a lie. I want to be with you longer. But Tarte and I live for you, dear brother. So go," Maha urged.

"...Sorry. No, thank you."

"You're welcome. I'm glad I was able to come here today. So this is where you and Tarte have been living. There are so many students, and they all look so radiant."

"Do you wish you were attending?" I questioned.

Any fourteen-year-old mage in Alvan could attend the academy if they applied. Maha was just as eligible as anyone else.

"Yes. I'm jealous of Tarte. Being a student sounds interesting, but more than that, I'm very, very envious that she gets to spend all her time with you... My wish to attend school with you is outweighed by my happiness at being of use from my place in Milteu.

I wanted to come, and I am jealous, but it's better the way things are now. I don't have any regrets."

Maha beamed. Her smile was always beautiful.

"...Thank you. I'll have to do something to thank you next time we meet."

"Yes, since I know now that you will indulge me to this degree, next time, I'll have to request something even more daring. But that's not important right now. You really don't have time. You need to go."

"Until next time."

"Bye, dear brother."

Leaving Maha and the café behind, I headed off to find Epona.

Maha's digging had uncovered the defining incident in Epona's life. Evidently, a key person in her life was resting in the city surrounding the academy.

Armed with that knowledge, I bought a particular item and headed for the public cemetery.

The graveyard was for knights who'd served in the capital. It was located in the same city as the school. A group of aristocrats had opposed the construction of a cemetery in the royal capital, so it'd been built here instead.

Differing offerings adorned the many graves.

Epona was kneeling before a monument devoted to multiple people. She'd bought that sky-blue dress she'd been staring at earlier and had placed in front of herself.

I walked up beside her, placed a bouquet of flowers in front of the structure, and put my hands together.

Epona looked at me with surprise plain on her face. Pretending not to notice, I knelt, offered a silent prayer, and stood back up.

"Didn't expect to see you here, Epona," I said once I'd finished.

"Yeah, what a coincidence. Is someone you knew buried here?" Epona asked.

"Yeah, a woman who was beloved among the knights of the Royal Order. I know she really liked flowers like these, and after I saw them at the Academy Market, I wanted to buy some for her."

"That's an amazing coincidence. The same thing happened to me with this sky-blue dress. She had an outfit just like this once and said she wanted me to wear it someday. Ah, wait, that's not what I meant. I don't like to dress in female clothing or anything."

One of the people entombed below the monument was someone significant to Epona. She'd been born in the rural region of Alvan that produced the colorful dye. That's why Epona had responded in such an unusual way upon spotting the vividly colored dress.

"Ha-ha, sounds like a weird person. My acquaintance also liked bright shades. She especially liked a flower called flaura. She always said they were the same color as her hometown."

"The same color as her home town…flaura… Your acquaintance isn't Mireille, is it?"

"It is. Did you know her, too?" I asked, feigning surprise.

Everything I was saying to Epona was a lie. I only knew Mireille from the documents Maha had assembled for me. It was all a ruse to earn Epona's trust.

"I'm actually also here to visit her grave. Wow, I never would've imagined you were a friend of hers. It really is a small world... Then there's something I need to tell you. If you were Mireille's friend, I need to apologize to you. I'm the one who killed her." Epona bowed her head to me, tears welling up in her eyes.

"You killed her? Do you mind telling me what you mean by that? I'd heard she perished in a fight against some monsters."

I shifted my outward facade to one of anger and doubt.

"That's wrong... Before I became the hero, I was a weakling without any mana. Everyone called me a failure. I couldn't do anything, and nobody wanted me. But then, one day, when a pack of monsters attacked my domain, power began to well up inside me. Before I knew it, I'd killed them all. After that, the Royal Order arrived. Mireille was the first one off that carriage. She told me I'm the hero and took me to the royal capital."

That much had been described in Maha's report.

"At the capital, I was officially proclaimed to be the hero. Mireille took charge of my instruction. She was very nice and pretty. Before becoming the hero, I hadn't received much of an education, so I learned a lot from her. She valued and praised me. In time, I started to think of Mireille as my older sister."

Epona clenched her fists tightly as she continued.

"It was all going so well. I was growing stronger and smarter every day. Mireille would praise me every time I took down a monster. I'd never been of help to anyone before, but now I was supporting everyone. It was comforting to know so many people needed me."

Epona's face was growing more distraught as she continued. Sadness and regret were written all over her face.

"I allowed myself to ride that wave of accomplishment and praise... And that's when it happened. It was the largest monster attack yet, and they weren't just great in number. They were strong, too. The Royal Order and I fought as best we could. As we fought, I noticed myself feeling more and more heated. Eventually, a strange feeling began to pool inside me. My vision then went red, and I lost myself. Lashing out with my power became too enjoyable for me to resist. I went on a rampage, and before I knew it, all the monsters were gone."

That battle was Epona's most lauded achievement. The monsters she'd defeated were strong enough to take out the entire Royal Order, but she'd reportedly repelled them with "minimal casualties."

"It wasn't until I regained my senses that I realized what I'd really done. I hadn't just destroyed the monsters. I'd attacked knights as well. Everyone had gotten hurt because of me—even Mireille. After searching for a while, I finally found her cold and covered in blood. The sight of her brought an urge to hit something to the forefront of my mind. In the next moment, I'd already done it. She was still breathing, and I tried to save her, but it was too late…"

Epona's words were both a lament and a confession.

The hero had the misfortune of being a regular person bestowed with incredible power. She didn't realize there was a bomb strapped to her back that could explode at any moment.

"What do you think the last thing Mireille said to me was, Lugh? Do you think that she said she didn't want to die? That she hated me?" Epona asked.

"I doubt it was any of those. The Mireille I know wouldn't have said those kinds of things," I replied.

"Ha-ha-ha, you're right. Mireille thanked me for defeating the monsters and told me I'd saved many people. The last thing she ever said to me was 'Protect the Alvanian Kingdom in my stead.'"

A large tear rolled down Epona's cheek.

"...I'm scared. The more serious I get in battle, the more enraged I become. If I wind up in another fight like that one, I could go off and kill someone again. I don't want to fight... But I can't run away. I owe it to Mireille not to. *'Protect the Alvanian Kingdom in my place.'* There's no way I can break that oath!!"

That was Epona's weakness. She was caught between a promise and a traumatic incident.

Combat terrified Epona, but it wasn't her own demise that filled her with dread. Instead, it was the concern that she'd slay another person who was dear to her. She'd loved Mireille like an older sister.

Unfortunately, Epona also felt an obligation to see Mireille's dying wish fulfilled. It was both a plea and a curse. Epona had no choice but to fight.

Mireille had probably asked that of Epona while fully understanding the implication. She'd known that if she didn't, the hero would never step foot on the battlefield again. To prevent that, Mireille had used the last of her power to keep Epona in the fight.

That woman had been a knight through and through. To the very last, she worked to ensure the safety of her kingdom.

I respected her unflinching sense of duty.

"Do you despise me for being the one who killed Mireille? Are you scared of me? Stay around me too long, and you might end up dead, too."

"No, I don't despise you. Even though you're frightened, you still try to keep your promise to Mireille... I finally understand why you were so happy when you said you thought I wouldn't get hurt sparring with you. It was because you don't want anyone to end up like Mireille ever again."

Epona wanted a training partner. She'd been searching for someone capable enough to survive her learning how to use her immense power without going berserk.

And she'd found me.

"Yeah. I'm very, very grateful to you. I want to become strong enough to resist losing myself when I fight. The thought of killing another person I love is too much. I don't know what I'll do if something like that happens again... I suppose you're not going to want to help me anymore, though. I killed your friend, after all."

This was the truth of Epona's heart. Without the key that was Mireille, I would've never unlocked it.

"I will support you as Mireille's friend. Mireille thanked you, didn't she? She asked you to protect Alvan. It's not my place to condemn you. To fulfill her wish... To help you become strong enough to protect this country, I will lend you my power. You don't need to worry. I'm strong enough to survive a few rounds with you. Feel free to train with me to your heart's content. Should you fall into bloodlust again on the battlefield, I will stop you," I declared.

"Can I trust you on that?"

"Yes. You know what I'm capable of."

"Yeah, I do. Um, there's something I've always wanted to say but couldn't bring myself to... Please be my friend. I never dared to say that to Mireille. If you're okay with someone like me, and I don't frighten you, then please be my friend... I'm lonely."

Overwhelming power meant overwhelming isolation. That was something I could never have predicted.

"Sounds good to me. We're friends," I agreed.

I extended my right hand for a handshake. Epona gripped it tightly and smiled as she wiped away her tears.

"Ah-ha-ha, I'm embarrassed, but happy, too. Thank you, Lugh."

"Of course, Epona."

And just like that, I became the hero's friend.

It was a relationship built on multiple calculated lies. Nonetheless, I still intended to be a genuine ally. That was how I planned to atone for deceiving Epona and using Mireille's name. I would make up for my falsehoods by saving the hero.

…It'd been hard to warm up to the hero before. After hearing her bare her heart to me, however, I really didn't want to kill her.

I didn't assassinate people like some mindless tool anymore. I'd vowed to live my life for myself. To that end, I needed to search as best I could for a way to save the world without slaying Epona.

I would use every method available to me to prevent things from reaching a point where I would be forced to choose between Epona and the rest of the world.

A few days had passed since the end of the Academy Market. I arrived in the classroom, and then while I was chatting with Naoise, an announcement sounded over the broadcast equipment.

"The following first-year students from Class S are to report to Visitation Room 2. Lugh, Naoise, Epona, Claudia, and Tarte. This is a top priority."

If they had called Naoise, Dia, Tarte, and me without Epona, this would likely have been about our secret mission. The hero had been called as well, however, so it had to be something unrelated.

"I wonder what it could be. This must be quite the emergency."

"We're missing class. I have a bad feeling about this."

Naoise and I looked at each other with bitter smiles on our faces. I hoped it wouldn't be anything too bothersome, but that seemed unlikely.

We entered the visitation room to find the instructor in charge of Class S, Professor Dune, and a dignified-looking woman in knight's clothing waiting for us. Decorations on the woman's uniform immediately informed us of her skill. Clearly, she held some sort of high position.

Professor Dune motioned for us to sit. Once we did so, he used a pen to mark a point on a map hung on the wall and began to speak.

"Apologies for causing you to miss your lessons. I'll get straight to the point. You five are being sent into combat. A village about five kilometers west of here is being encroached upon by a horde of around one hundred orcs. Orcs use human women for breeding. If left to their own devices, the orcs will multiply and attack the nearby city of Rutolia. We must avoid that outcome at all costs. We're going to set up an ambush and wipe them out before they have a chance to do anything to the village."

Monsters had been appearing in larger numbers lately. These portentous events foretold the return of the Demon King. I'd been expecting something like this to happen sooner or later.

Our professor laid out a sensible and straightforward battle strategy.

The city of Rutolia was the economic center of this region, and it couldn't be allowed to fall. While Rutolia possessed strong defenses in the form of heavily fortified walls, the hope was that we would stop the orcs before sealing off the city became a necessity.

However, three things were bothering me, and I raised my hand.

"Lugh Tuatha Dé. You may speak," Professor Dune allowed.

"I have a few questions. There should be a stronghold in front of the village. Does the orcs' advance on the village mean they managed to break through the stronghold unharmed?"

"No. The orcs didn't push past the stronghold. It seems they simply appeared beyond its perimeter. Unfortunately, the bastion has its hands full dealing with another group of monsters, so they won't be able to offer any help."

"Okay, my second question: No matter how strong we are, we are students. It hasn't been very long since we enrolled, and we haven't received much training in military strategy. Could you please share the reason for entrusting us with this duty despite our inexperience?"

I didn't lack confidence, but I still wanted to know why five first-years had been chosen. We had power to spare, but we weren't coordinated as a group to move effectively as a unit. Sending us into battle seemed abnormal.

"The honest answer is we're simply shorthanded. When there are monsters that need exterminating, the duty is first entrusted to the infested domain's ruler. If they are not able to deal with it, they request help from the Royal Order. Lately, monsters have repeatedly been appearing in large quantities, and the Royal Order has sent out all personnel not needed to defend the capital. When the knights cannot deal with a situation, professors and upper-level students are dispatched from the academy. As you may have already surmised, all available professors and upper-level students are away. You five are the only first-years the faculty feels can handle this responsibility."

It seems like they think very highly of us.

I'd never seen an orc in person, but I knew it was suicide for anyone other than a mage to take them on. Suppose the knights from the Royal Order and the upperclassmen were already off handling other problems. In that case, I could understand why the academy would want to send novice mages like us over ordinary folk with military training.

"Okay, now for my third question: We are going to be fighting orcs. Considering the worst-case scenario, it'd be best if girls weren't around. Would it not be best to leave Dia and Tarte behind?"

"You're exactly right. However, I'll say this: They'll be fine if you protect them. The scale of this horde is huge, and we can't afford to send any fewer than five people. Even considering the risks, we need to make sure we meet the enemy with the proper amount of force."

I felt an urge to ask Professor Dune if he'd lost his mind.

Orcs were giants that stood around three meters tall, and they had the strength to match their bulk. They also had a unique method of reproduction. Orcs were an all-male species, and they reproduced by impregnating females of other species.

Orcs were incredibly fertile, and they could continue to copulate for more than half a day. Uninterrupted, they would impregnate a female in a single night. The child was born only three days later. It was the offspring that was the most problematic.

Orc children inherited the best traits of their mothers' species. An orc attack not only increased their numbers, but those born of human mothers would possess higher intelligence. If those intelligent orcs took command of the horde, their threat level would increase exponentially.

If things went south for us...

"If Tarte and Dia end up impregnated, they will give birth to terrifyingly strong monsters," I said.

"Don't make me repeat myself. We are aware of the risks. I'm telling you not to let that happen."

Because orcs received their mothers' most valuable qualities, an orc born from a powerful mage would be both smart and mighty in battle.

...The last thing I wanted to do was take Dia and Tarte to a location brimming with creatures that were filled with lust for human women.

"Thank you very much for worrying about me, my lord. But I will be fine. I won't let them beat me," Tarte assured.

"That's right. You've trained us well, Lugh, and you'll be there to protect us if something goes wrong. This is going to be a tough job, and I want to help you," Dia insisted.

I can't bring myself to think that optimistically.

Our enemy was powerful. Orcs had immense strength and endless stamina. There was a decent chance something could go wrong.

"No matter what you may have to say, the order is absolute. You all are nobles of this country. You should give your all to serve it... I will be accompanying you for support, and this lady from the Royal Order will be traveling with us as well," Professor Dune explained.

"Apologies for the delay in introducing myself. I am Rachel Barton. I was a member of this academy's very first class. I will protect you all, so you do not need to worry."

Rachel Barton. She was one of the first graduates of this academy and probably graduated with top honors.

We five took turns giving our names to her.

"I've heard that multiple once-a-decade talents have entered the academy this year. I've been looking forward to meeting you," Rachel said with a smile.

"We will work hard to live up to your expectations," I responded, deciding to concede to Professor Dune's orders. No matter what excuses I made, the decision had been set.

"With Lugh and me on the job, we'll be just fine. What's more, the hero is coming, too. It doesn't matter how many orcs there are; we'll win," Naoise declared. I couldn't hide my discomfort with such an overconfident statement.

While I didn't say anything about it out loud, there was something even more concerning than our opponents—Epona. I'd fought her many times since our first sparring session. If she went berserk, I don't think anyone would escape unharmed except myself.

If Epona could lose it during a mock battle, then the risk of an outburst during a real fight with actual monsters seemed even higher. Not even I was sure what'd happen if Epona went on a rampage.

Epona turned to me and said, "I'll do my best. You've really helped me get more confident, Lugh!"

That's exactly why I'm scared. I'll have to watch out for Epona as much as the orcs.

"That is all. Departure is in three hours. Prepare yourselves, then gather at the Royal Order's carriage in the main square. This is a military operation, so you must wear a uniform. That is all; you're dismissed." Professor Dune turned his back to us as if to convey he had nothing left to disclose.

Never had I guessed I'd be assigned duty so early in my tenure at the academy.

We walked into the hallway and then headed to our rooms to prepare. Dia and Tarte remained with me. Naoise had an ambitious smile on his face as he walked away.

Facing Dia and Tarte, I cautioned, "There are three promises you need to make me, or you may not survive. I couldn't say any of this in front of the professor or the knight."

Seeing how serious I was, they both nodded with firm expressions.

"First, stay close to me. Don't pursue any enemies too far away and stay by my side. Understand? Anything could happen once we engage our opponents. A blow from an orc will knock you unconscious regardless of how much you've strengthened yourself with mana. They instinctively prioritize overpowering females and taking them away. If any one of them succeeds in grabbing a girl, the other orcs will form a wall to protect them. We need to make sure that doesn't happen. As long as you two are by my side, I will cover your blind spots."

"O-okay. I promise to stay close to you," Tarte agreed.

"Yeah, I'll be careful, too. I don't like being separated from you anyway," Dia added.

"Second, prioritize my orders. When the professor's orders run counter to mine, follow my orders without hesitation," I instructed.

"That goes without saying. I am your retainer."

Such an attitude made Tarte unsuitable as a knight of the academy, but it was a perfect answer for my servant.

"I don't have anything cool to say like Tarte, but I also plan to do as you say," Dia replied.

"Lastly, we need to watch out for Epona. She's a far greater danger than the orcs. Don't let your guard down...or you will die."

As long as they keep those three promises, they'll be fine.

Using brand new students like us was a clear demonstration of how shorthanded the school was.

I wondered if the academy had constructed this situation to test the hero's abilities. It hardly mattered now. All that was left was to give it my all. Anything less risked death.

My preparations took little time, but I arrived at the gathering point to find everyone else already there.

Epona was so strong that she didn't need equipment, but the others were dressed for battle.

Naoise had a magic sword, and while Tarte, Dia, and I looked no different than usual, we were wearing special undergarments.

They'd been made from monster tissue that had been extracted using Tuatha Dé medical secrets. The material guarded exceptionally well against slashing and bludgeoning attacks, as well as heat. It was quite malleable, too. Tuatha Dé assassins wore outfits made of this wondrous stuff when entering a rough combat situation.

"This is uncomfortably tight on my chest."

"…Do your best to hang in there."

Evidently, the undergarments hadn't been designed with the chest size of someone like Tarte in mind. While they had some amount of elasticity, it was not without limit. I felt bad for Tarte, but there was nothing to be done.

"What? That's cr—I mean, y-yeah… Lugh, I don't think it's gonna be easy for me, either," Dia piped up.

"I-is that so?"

Dia was clearly lying. Her chest fit just fine.

Before long, it was time for us to depart. We all climbed into the wagon and took off for our destination.

The horde of orcs didn't seem like it was going to be too much of a problem. I only hoped the army's information was correct.

We arrived at the ravine where we were going to ambush the orcs. Some soldiers were gathered there, too.

Non-mages were unable to fight in battles against monsters. Still, they could serve as lookouts, scouts, or guards. Other tasks like making camp, assisting with villager evacuation, procuring supplies, and delivering messages to and from command could also be entrusted to them.

Their presence enabled mages to focus on battle.

A scout returned and reported to Rachel. The woman nodded, then looked like she was contemplating how best to convey this new information to us. After considering for a moment, she sauntered over.

"The orcs will arrive in four hours. We don't know how, but their numbers have increased. The estimate has increased from one hundred to one hundred and fifty," she told us with a calm voice. An increase of 50 percent was not good news. Typically, the proper procedure would've been to cancel our operation and retreat.

I waited for Rachel to say something else, but she remained quiet. Tarte then broke the silence by hesitantly raising her hand.

"Um, is there a plan for this?"

"The plan is simple. We use this ravine to kill all the orcs. To be more specific, those who are skilled in close combat will fight hard up front, and those who are skilled at using mana will fire spells from the rear," Rachel replied.

Doesn't sound like much of a plan. That said, giving us a complicated strategy when we held no real organized combat training was impossible.

"Miss Rachel, I have something to say. The canyon is a suitable place to engage the orcs, but the road leading into it is too wide. Fighting an army of one hundred and fifty head-on would be suicide," I observed.

The entrance into the ravine was wide enough that five to six orcs could enter at a time. Handling that many was an impossible task for our vanguard. It would lead to our rearguard getting surrounded, which would keep them from casting spells. In the end, we were just too few.

"But we don't have any better options," Rachel protested.

"Perhaps if you consider the map to be stagnant, but what if we change the terrain? Dia and I can use our earth magic to narrow the road. We can make a gently sloping dirt wall so no more than two orcs will be able to pass through at a time," I suggested.

I drew a simple picture on a piece of paper. Just as I'd explained, we'd alter the landscape by creating a slope in the earth that connected the walls of the canyon. This would make a choke point that reduced how many orcs could get through. The barricade would also keep enemy projectiles out. The mages in the rearguard would be safe to hurl spells over our wall.

In truth, I would've preferred to close off the ravine entirely, but that would incentivize the orcs to look for another way around, so the opening had to be kept wide enough that they still wanted to go through.

"That's an interesting plan. But do you have enough mana to create a dirt wall of this size?" Rachel inquired.

"That won't be a problem for Dia and me. You said we have four hours until the enemy arrives, right? We'll build the wall and still have enough time left over to recover any lost mana," I declared.

"I agree completely," added Dia.

Rachel looked at Professor Dune.

"I'll allow it. Lugh, Claudia, give it a try."

"Yes, sir."

"Lugh, let's do our best."

Dia and I nodded at each other and immediately got to work.

The mages and the non-mages alike looked on in wonder.

"This is magnificent. I'm always amazed by the beauty of Lugh and Dia's magic," said Naoise.

"Yes, Lord Lugh and Lady Dia are geniuses when it comes to magic," responded Tarte.

"Whoa, that's incredible. I can't believe those two are students. I wish I could hire them into my service right now," Rachel admitted.

While we weren't using any spells of our own design, our near-perfect execution despite the massive scale and our seemingly endless supplies of mana must've made us look inhuman.

But that aside, are Rachel and the professor right in the head? If I hadn't said anything, the fight could've gone very badly. Everyone but Epona undoubtedly would've died.

Once again, I was left to wonder if they'd done this on purpose as a way to gauge the hero's strength.

◇

After our construction project came to an end, we left the watch to the troops and went to rest in our tent. To have Dia recover mana more quickly, I induced sleep using a Tuatha Dé secret drug that caused muscle relaxation and an accelerated stamina recovery rate.

"I'm getting nervous, my lord," Tarte said, her hands shaking.

"Are you scared?" I asked.

"No. I'm never scared when I'm with you."

"Is that so? I have one piece of advice for you. Make sure you don't hesitate. Act with certainty."

"Okay!"

Tarte gripped her spear. Expecting a tough battle, she was reinforcing the weapon's joints.

"Also, um, can you give me a little? I've run out again," Tarte admitted.

"You still can't control your eye?" I inquired.

"Yes, I'm leaking mana constantly. So please give me some of yours, my lord."

I glanced over at Dia. It looked like she was fast asleep. That meant we didn't need to move somewhere else.

Tuatha Dé eyes had a disadvantage. While they strengthened your vision by gathering mana, you needed practice to keep yourself from unconsciously feeding mana to them. If you weren't careful, they could run you dry.

For that reason, I had to use a spell to refill Tarte's mana.

I pressed my lips against Tarte's. Using that as an entry point, I poured mana into her. It was easiest to transfer mana through contact of mucous membranes.

When my lips touched hers, Tarte collapsed into my arms. She closed her eyes and pressed hard against me. When mana began to flow into Tarte's body, she shivered, and her breathing intensified.

The spell was one of my own design. Connecting mana wavelengths was an extremely advanced technique. I don't think more than a handful of people had ever attempted it.

...I didn't really want to use this method, but ever since I'd used it to save Tarte from mana depletion one time, she'd gotten into the habit of pestering me for it.

Truthfully, I suspected that Tarte had been able to control her eye for a while, and she was just using this as an excuse. She looked adorable when she asked, however, so I allowed it. Plus, holding her tight and pressing my lips against hers was enjoyable.

"Is that enough?" I asked, breaking away from Tarte.

After the spell, Tarte always seemed to grow more amorous than you might've expected of someone like her.

"Yes, I'm full of your mana, and I feel so brave now!" Tarte brought a hand to her lips with an ecstatic expression on her face.

...I kept this method of recovery a secret from Dia. If I told her about it, it would likely mean trouble.

The camp suddenly grew noisy. The enemy had arrived.

"Sounds like it's time. Dia, wake up."

"Mmmm, good morning, Lugh."

"I did tell you to rest up, but sleeping that soundly in this kind of situation takes some guts."

"I guess so. But thanks to that nap, I recovered a lot of mana."

Dia was acting no different than normal. It didn't look like she'd seen what Tarte and I had just done.

"Then let's go. Dia, you still have what I gave you, right?" I asked.

"Of course."

Dia pulled five Fahr Stones filled to their critical point out of her pouch.

They were the last resort in case she ran out of mana. Fahr Stones were something I really wanted to keep secret, but Dia's life was more valuable.

"Tarte, are you ready?"

"Yes, I won't let them beat me."

The soldiers came to get us. The time had come for battle.

The sun was sinking low into the horizon, and everyone was in their places.

Naoise, Tarte, and Epona were the vanguard.

I was stationed as the middle guard. My job was to take out orcs with magic and then support the vanguard if anything went wrong. Dia was in the back, focusing on ranged spells.

Farther behind her, Rachel and Professor Dune were waiting in reserve. Their role was to assist us if we fell into a dangerous situation and to stop any orcs that broke through. They were also standing ready to replace anyone who became unable to continue the battle.

"The orcs are here."

What little I could see through the gaps in the choke point that Dia and I had created was painted dark green with the skin of the approaching monsters.

Regular soldiers had been stationed above the ravine to make up for our limited visibility. They would report on any unusual movement.

The three-meter-tall giants marched through the canyon. Soldiers from above fired arrows, but the thick-skinned orcs suffered no injury.

Just as we'd intended, the monsters were slowed by the mass of earth Dia and I had constructed. As soon as Dia and I were assured of that, we began our incantations.

We finished our spells the moment the first orcs passed through the entrance. Both of us cried out, *"Crimson Explosion!"*

Crimson Explosion was the twentieth fire spell bestowed by the gods upon repeated use of fire magic. Most mages died before ever learning it. As you might've expected, it was very powerful.

Fireballs the size of basketballs flew over the wall in parabolic arcs, landing amid the horde of orcs and exploding. Red flames roared to life amid the army of monsters.

A soldier observing from above called out, "The spells made impact! Eight enemies are down!"

Orcs really were tough. Despite being elite mages, Dia and I only took out four orcs each using an advanced spell.

However, we didn't have time to despair. Our role as mages was to use the wall as a shield to launch as many spells as we could. The more orcs we took out, the easier a time the vanguard would have.

Of course, the vanguard's role was to eliminate any orcs that passed through the entrance. They were intercepting the first two orcs that managed to get through right now.

Epona charged at one of them.

"Die!"

She simply rushed up to it and swung with the back of her fist. Its abdomen rippled and then ruptured. Its top half was cleaved from its bottom half and was sent flying, wedging into the dirt wall.

Epona didn't use weapons. Her strength rendered weapons unusable because they couldn't handle the force of her attacks and ended up breaking.

"Let's go, Tarte!"

"Okay!"

Naoise and Tarte engaged the other orc together. It was an improvised attack, but they skillfully trapped the monster by flanking it. While the orc was unsure of what to do, Tarte pierced an eye with her spear, and Naoise sliced off a hand with his sharp sword.

That was skilled. Orcs were protected by thick, armor-like skin and fat. Any normal attack couldn't damage them. Despite that, Tarte had taken out an eye, and Naoise easily cut through the creature's wrist, leaving a growing pool of red fluid. Despite the blood loss, the orc continued to rage until it collapsed less than a minute later and went cold.

At the rate things were going, we would be able to defeat the orcs without overextending ourselves. As long as they used the path we'd created, no more than two, at most three, of the monsters would be able to get through at a time. Epona, Naoise, and Tarte could handle such an amount without issue. As they took care of the orcs up front, Dia and I burned those caught waiting at the choke point.

It was going to be an intense fight, but our victory was inevitable. All we had to do was maintain our current pattern. The only uncertainty was whether we'd be able to take out all the orcs before we ran out of strength.

And so began a test of endurance.

Thirty minutes flew by, but our fight had still not concluded. Something felt unusual.

We should've taken out more than one hundred orcs by now, yet the onslaught showed no signs of letting up.

The wall kept us from seeing the whole picture, forcing us to rely on reports from the soldiers above on the sides of the canyon.

Naoise yelled at the soldiers, rare frustration breaking through his usual calm demeanor. "How many more of them can there possibly be?!"

"By our estimation, one hundred and twenty!" came the reply.

"What do you mean? We've already killed at least a hundred of them!" Naoise exclaimed.

"They're getting reinforcements from somewhere."

An extra fifty had been bad enough, but now there were sizable reserves.

Altogether, the orc force totaled two hundred twenty. What's worse, we had no guarantee the number would stop there.

An extra seventy soldiers is too great a number for them to have just been hiding out somewhere... I have a bad feeling about this. We should consider the possibility that there is a demon with the power to produce monsters lurking nearby. This is bad.

"Sorry, I don't think I can last any longer."

Looking pale, Dia fell to her knees. She'd run out of mana.

It wasn't surprising. She'd been casting Crimson Explosion continuously for over half an hour.

Tarte was in trouble as well. Her movements were visibly slowing.

An orc swung at her with its club, and she failed to dodge.

"GAAAHHHHHHH!"

Tarte just barely managed to defend herself with her left arm, but her bone broke with a snap, and she was knocked backward onto the ground. It didn't seem like she was able to stand back up.

An orc turned toward Tarte and reached out toward her. It was going to carry her away.

"You stinking pig!!!"

I stopped my Crimson Explosion incantation and sprinted toward her. I charged and used my momentum to spin in the air, landing with a palm strike that sent the orc flying.

It was the same move I'd used on the vice-commander of the Royal Guard during the entrance exam. It caused an explosion of mana and energy within the orc, ripping a hole through the creature. It bled out and died.

Unlike the last time I'd used the maneuver, I didn't hold back. This caused an explosion within the monster that allowed me to ignore its thick fat and muscle.

"Lord Lugh!"

"Tarte, fall back. I'm taking your place in the vanguard."

"I can still fight."

"No, you can't! If you can stand, then get up and withdraw."

Tarte stopped arguing. Doubtless she understood that she was a hindrance now.

I'd trained her better than to fail after only thirty minutes, but she was likely still adjusting to her Tuatha Dé eye. It'd worn her out.

I took Tarte's place in the vanguard. While covering Tarte behind me, I turned toward an orc.

Tarte fought her hardest against a terrifying slew of enemies. I'll have to praise her later.

"If you're moving up here, who will take out the orcs in the back?" asked Naoise.

"If I don't fight up here, the vanguard will break. I'll fill in until Rachel and the professor get here."

"We've been fighting our butts off. It's about time they come and take our place."

Naoise's words were in jest, but I couldn't deny he had it hard. He'd been fighting at the vanguard for half an hour.

Things only got worse from there.

Dia, pale-faced and on her knees, shrieked, "Lugh, our wall!"

"Guess that was all the punishment it could take."

The orcs stuck outside the ravine hadn't been waiting patiently in line. All the while, they'd been trying to smash our barricade.

That alone may not have been enough to bring it down. Unfortunately, Epona had unknowingly weakened the earthen structure with all her smashing.

The battle would have ended before the wall crumbled if the orcs' numbers hadn't increased from the original estimate. The fight was dragging on longer than Dia and I had built the wall to last. It was only a few moments from collapsing. We'd been too optimistic.

The orcs surged into the barricade. It collapsed, enabling us to see that the orcs' numbers hadn't changed at all since the beginning of the battle. With nothing to stop them, orcs charged in six at a time.

I'd known this was a possibility, but it was still a crushing blow to my morale.

We stood no chance against so many orcs at once. Dia and Tarte were also out of commission.

I couldn't afford to hold back. If I didn't use my full strength here, we were all going to die. I grabbed one of the Fahr Stones I'd brought as a last resort, and then it happened.

"Finally, a chance to rage to my heart's content. Every. Last. One of you little *goddamn maggots* is so *annoyinggggg*. I'm going to kill you all!!"

An enraged Epona charged into the horde of orcs, which for most people would've only led to getting surrounded and beaten to a pulp. However, she just tossed the monsters aside as she laughed.

The giggling felt far more sinister than jovial. There was a distinct bloodlust to it.

This was what happened to Epona when, as she put it, her vision went red.

Naoise's face stiffened, and Tarte and Dia cowered. Taking no notice of our stares, the savage beast that was the hero began to tear into its prey.

Epona had no trouble overpowering the orcs. She beat them beyond recognition with nothing but her bare fists and the occasional fireball.

This isn't a battle—it's a one-sided slaughter.

Orcs were incapable of knowing fear, though, so they continued to throw themselves at Epona despite her clear advantage.

"Ah-ha-ha-ha, what the hell, th-there's no way she's even the same species as us. Why didn't she just do that from the beginning? Epona would have been fine on her own. There was no reason for us even to be here," said a shaking Naoise, struggling to force out the words.

Naoise had seen me fight Epona in mock battles many times, but this was the first time he'd seen Epona get serious, and her impossible strength left him trembling.

"Yeah, really. We could have sent in Epona alone, and they would've been wiped out a while ago without the need for any strategy," I remarked.

"It sounds like you knew she could do this beforehand. If that's the case, then why did you come up with all this—?"

Naoise was interrupted by an orc's head that came flying toward us like a speeding bullet.

It was only because of the extra mana I'd put into my Tuatha

Dé eyes that I could evade. I used my knife's handle to deflect the incoming head, and it ended up embedded deep into the natural wall behind us.

If I'd tried to catch that, I would've lost an arm. That's why I'd had no choice but to redirect the severed head. A direct hit would've seriously injured me, mage or not. Epona's strength was so great that she'd sent a skull speeding at lethal velocity.

"That's your answer. Fighting orcs is significantly less scary than getting caught up in a battle with Epona. I wanted to avoid a situation where Epona needed to get serious. Don't let your guard down," I cautioned.

"I just want to get out of here as fast as I can," Naoise replied.

"Even with Epona going all out, deserting could lead to trouble. If running were permissible, I would've already done so," I admitted.

I looked behind me to see Dia and Tarte resting on the ground, neither in any condition to defend herself. Until those two were safe, I had to protect them.

No matter how strong Epona was, she couldn't deal with that many orcs all at once. Some of them were going to get past her. That was another reason I couldn't leave.

Speak of the devil, here come some of the monsters now.

Two of the towering green creatures had slipped around Epona. Naoise and I gave each other a look, but Epona moved in before we could intercept the orcs.

"You piece of shit pigs! You think you can run from me?!"

Mana gathered in her right hand. Without an incantation, Epona launched a simple blast of magical power at one of the monsters.

Spells were mana given a kind of shape. The energy alone

didn't have much attack power. If using simple mana blasts was an effective method of attack, no one would've bothered with spells because of the incantation time required.

However, Epona's attack had a colossal amount of power behind it, further strengthened by all of her S-Rank hero skills.

"No!"

That blast of mana was on course to hit the orc directly. Unfortunately, Dia and Tarte were right behind it. Epona's attack would consume the monster and then continue and strike Dia and Tarte. Weakened as they were, they had no hope of dodging.

I jumped to the side, putting myself between the girls and the orc.

Should I use the full strength that I've been concealing at the academy? If I do that, I can block this without taking any damage... No, I can handle this without doing that.

I decided to continue concealing my full power, even if it risked me getting hurt.

Gathering mana, I hardened my monster-tissue underclothes. They were double layered. One was capable of stiffening to resist attacks, while the other was soft to absorb any impact. Pouring mana into the suit made it the ultimate defense.

Epona's blast pierced through the orc as easily as I'd anticipated, and I caught it with my back.

My shoulders broke. I'd braced myself as best I could but was still sent flying through the air.

Overall, I'd taken it quite well. Ending up with only a few broken bones after stopping an attack from the hero was something to take pride in. My Rapid Recovery would mend my wounds in only a few minutes. I needed to change my trajectory, however. I was headed right for Dia and Tarte.

I turned Epona's clump of mana toward the ground and fired it, using it to change my direction as I soared through the air. This altered my fall enough that I wasn't going to land on the girls.

Unfortunately, I was definitely going to snap another bone or two when I hit the ground, but I didn't mind that level of injury.

"Lord Lugh!"

Tarte got up and dashed forward to catch me, despite her ragged, mana-deficient state.

I crashed into her, and we both tumbled along the ground for a fair distance. When we at last came to a stop, Tarte was unconscious and bleeding from the mouth.

"Tarte!"

Why did she catch me?! She had to have known this would happen if she snatched me out of the air without any mana to strengthen herself.

It was an incredibly boneheaded thing to do. Tarte had only done it because she'd wanted to protect me. That was the sort of person she was.

I looked up and met Epona's eyes. An expression of fear formed on her face after she looked at me.

She didn't look anything like the battle rager from a moment ago. It was clear she was slowing down, but it hardly mattered. The orcs couldn't so much as scratch her, even if they came at her with everything they had.

"I—I, I never intended… I didn't mean to…," Epona whimpered, begging me to believe her.

I understood that much. I blamed myself more than Epona. I'd known this could happen, and I'd formed a plan I thought would've been able to deal with it.

I was also conceited enough to believe that I could handle

that blast of mana while keeping my own abnormally high power a secret. That arrogance had been what'd left Tarte collapsed on the ground. Knowing Tarte, I should've expected her to try to help me.

"I'll do what I can to take out the ones that get through. Turn back around and fight!" I finally forced out.

I really should've said something like "Don't worry about it. It was an accident." I just couldn't manage it, though. Seeing Tarte bloody and beaten had left me unable to think straight.

If I consoled Epona now, it would've sounded contrived. So that was all I could get myself to say.

After another fifteen minutes of fighting, the orcs were all dead. Our job done, we began to head back to the academy.

Epona wasn't at quite the same level after the incident with Tarte, but she'd still been far beyond anything the orc army could've handled. More orcs slipped past her, but Professor Dune and Rachel finally stepped in to help.

What concerned me was that as soon as Epona started using her full power, the orcs' numbers curiously waned. They'd been spawning infinitely from some unknown location until that point. Again, I had to consider the possibility that this had all been staged to gauge Epona's capabilities.

Perhaps it's a demon trying to learn what they're up against and use that information to take her down. If we assume they threw away that many orcs as a sacrifice, then just how great is their real fighting strength?

I shook my head. This was hardly the time to be thinking about such things. Tarte's treatment had to come first.

"Lugh, will Tarte be okay?" Dia asked worriedly.

"She'll be fine. She has some bruises, bone fractures, and scratches, but I can heal all of that."

"Thank goodness. I was worried after how far she flew through the air."

We had a war doctor with us in the carriage, but I was more skilled, so I handled Tarte's treatment. After taking care of anything that required immediate attention, I used my mana to strengthen her self-healing.

"Tarte's complexion is looking much better," Dia observed.

"Yeah, there's no need to worry anymore," I replied.

I patted Tarte on the head.

The curtain separating the bed from the other seats then opened.

"Um, I—I need to apologize," Epona stated, avoiding my eyes all the while.

"...It was a very intense battle. It wasn't your fault," I assured.

Having sorted out my feelings, I finally let Epona know that I wasn't upset with her.

"But I—I really hurt Tarte," protested the hero.

"If you apologize, Tarte will forgive you."

"I hope so. Um, sorry for injuring you too, Lugh. I let it happen again. Every time I fight on a battlefield, my vision goes red, and then I start to rage, and before I know it I've hurt everybody, so, so I..."

Epona's fists were shaking.

"I wanted to change. I wanted to become strong enough to keep a clear head even in that wild state. After no one got hurt during our mock battles, I thought things would be okay today, but sure enough, it happened again..."

I'd been helping Epona ever since that promise during the Academy Festival after she'd opened up to me. Every time one of our sparring sessions ended safely, Epona got a little more confident.

"Also, I thought you'd be able to stop me if I lost control. Ah-ha-ha, I guess that was assuming too much. I'm sorry for that, too. I'm really not cut out to be the hero."

With that final comment, Epona returned to her seat.

Dia gave a strained laugh.

"She doesn't seem like a bad girl. She also thinks extremely highly of you."

"Yeah."

...She thought I would be able to stop her.

I thought back to what Epona and I had talked about during the Academy Market. I'd sworn not to die at her side and that I'd stop her if she ever lost control. Unfortunately, I'd failed. I'd chosen to conceal my full strength, and something terrible nearly happened.

"Dia, do you think I should apologize to Epona? I didn't say anything too harsh, but I let my frustration over not being able to protect Tarte affect my attitude. I glared at her after Tarte lost consciousness," I said.

"The Lugh I know would apologize," Dia replied immediately.

"You're right. I'll apologize once she's calmed down."

I'd known the whole time that I was in the wrong here. It seemed I had some room for improvement. I'd grown more human in my second life, but that had allowed immaturity to affect my behavior.

I need to concentrate on one thing at a time.

"I should tell Tarte I'm sorry, too," I thought aloud.

"If you feel for her, one kiss will do the trick, you know. That'll be all it takes to put her in a good mood," Dia remarked.

"You're right. That's what I'll do," I decided.

"Huh, I meant that as a joke, but you took it seriously?! You didn't hesitate at all there, did you?! Have you and Tarte already been kissing?!" Dia exclaimed.

"...No we haven't."

Those mana-replenishing kisses were a secret.

"That's not fair; you should kiss me, too. You haven't kissed me at all recently, Lugh."

For the rest of the ride back to the academy, Dia probed me about how far Tarte and I had gotten. Tarte woke up after we arrived, and before I could express my remorse to her, she apologized fervently to me. She even refused my offer to make it up to her. That being the case, I decided to give her a surprise present after a week or two.

I also had to seek out Epona and tell her I was sorry first thing tomorrow. The sooner that kind of thing was taken care of, the better.

Unfortunately, I ended up not being able to apologize to Epona.

I had planned to catch her before classes began the day following the battle with the orcs. However, she'd already been summoned for another mission and had departed the academy. Unlike last time, Epona had gone off alone on this assignment. Naoise, Tarte, Dia, and I hadn't even been told about it.

…The academy probably thinks less highly of us after that battle with the orcs.

Dia, Tarte, and I had lunch out in the courtyard. Tarte was humming as she poured us some tea.

"Are you sure you're feeling better? I asked.

"Yes. You treated me all night long, my lord, so I'm in perfect shape."

Tarte flexed her arms to prove her point. As she'd said, I'd stayed up until morning, speeding up her recovery and healing her injuries. Still, I was surprised to see how unruffled Tarte was. Wounds as bad as hers should've at least left her feeling tired. That bothered me more than any of her physical injuries.

Despite everything that'd happened, Tarte got up early and made our lunches as she always did. Even her mood seemed unaffected.

"Are you sure you're okay?" I pressed.

"Yes, I've never been better. I embarrassed myself yesterday. I'll train even harder to prevent that from happening again! I need to master the eye you gave me," she replied.

Whether enthusiasm or mana, I couldn't say, but Tarte's one Tuatha Dé eye shone visibly from behind its colored contact lens.

"I wonder if I'll ever get those eyes," Dia said, gazing at Tarte's right eye in obvious jealousy.

"I'll have to think about it. Tuatha Dé eyes are indeed useful, but you leak mana until you get used to them. You have a lot of mana, Dia, but the eyes might run you dry in a battle like yesterday's. I'm not sure they'd suit you," I explained.

"Hmm, yeah, I might not have mana to spare for the eyes at first, but I can learn to control it through practice, right? They're also significantly better than normal eyes even when not enhanced by mana," reasoned Dia.

"That's true," I replied.

"Then I do want them. If I get those eyes, I'll have to get used to them as soon as possible. By the way, there's something I don't get. Even though Tarte has way less mana than me, I've never seen her collapse. She's used to managing the eye now, but if she was leaking mana before, then how come she never had any trouble?"

Dia noticed. Can't say I'm surprised.

"Oh, that? Lord Lugh has been regularly replenishing my mana. I've gotten much better at controlling the eye recently, though, so he hasn't been doing it as often," Tarte admitted.

Dia turned to me and smiled. Something was terrifying about that expression.

...This is bad.

I'd told Tarte not to tell anyone about the mana transfer spell because it was a secret House Tuatha Dé technique. I'd foolishly forgotten Dia was now part of the family and therefore privy to its knowledge.

"Hey, Lugh. I've never heard of a method capable of replenishing someone's magical power. If you can do that sort of thing, why didn't you use it on me during the battle yesterday? If you had, I would've been able to keep fighting."

"Because it's Tuatha Dé confidential information. I can't just do it out in the open," I shot back.

"Hmmm... But how would you do something like that in the first place? Linking mana wavelengths would be difficult to pull off, but not impossible... Even Lugh's precise control of mana would probably drop to around twenty percent. Ah, but that wouldn't matter with his near-limitless mana. The problem would be the method of transmission. Direct contact would be essential... To increase transmission efficiency and prevent the mana from transforming after the wavelengths are joined, that would be the only choice... I see how it is. Hmph, it's not fair that you've only been doing that with Tarte."

Dia was terrifying. She'd figured it all out after merely hearing I'd been replenishing Tarte's mana.

"So, Lugh. I've been wanting to practice advanced spells that use a lot of magic power, but because advanced spells drain me very quickly, I never make much progress. I've been stuck," Dia said.

"Got it. I'll supply you with as much mana as you want," I agreed, taking the hint.

"Yay! Hmm-hmm. I can't wait. I can practice magic to my heart's content and kiss Lugh at the same time... If you're reluctant to do it that way, there is another method of direct mucous membrane contact we can use," proposed Dia.

"You can't do that until you get married!" interrupted a deeply blushing Tarte.

While Tarte wasn't used to talking about that sort of thing, she still understood what Dia had been suggesting.

That method is actually more efficient, but I'll keep quiet about that.

"Well, actually, let's not use that one. I don't want to upset Tarte. I'm also a little scared of it, so just keep it as something to look forward to in the future. Please kiss me to supply me with mana for now," Dia decided.

It seemed I had no way out of this.

It's not that I didn't like kissing. I loved Dia, and kissing her was great, but there was a reason I'd been avoiding restoring her mana.

Namely, I knew it would be difficult to stop myself if I started up with her. Kissing Dia and stopping there was sure to be agony. Young bodies were so challenging to control.

"Back to what we were talking about before. You want those eyes, don't you, Dia?" I asked.

"Of course. The ability to see mana would make controlling magic much easier. There is no doubt I would get better at spellcasting. You can normally only feel mana, so that would be very helpful. Detecting gathering magical power would also be useful to read the flow of battle from the rearguard. That's likely to be my main use for them."

Spoken like a real sorcerer. Being able to see mana was just as big of a boon as seeing objects moving at high speeds.

"All right, I'll get ready for both of your surgeries," I declared.

Thus it was determined that I would not only give Tarte her remaining Tuatha Dé eye, but I would also provide a pair to Dia. I was looking forward to seeing how this enhanced their growth.

Epona returned a week later and began avoiding me at every turn. It wasn't just me, either. She also kept her distance from Dia and Tarte.

There was no doubting that something had happened while she was off on her solo mission.

I'd tried to approach Epona on multiple occasions, but she always ran away. She'd been skipping our study group, too. Left with no other choice, I decided to visit her room at night. If things continued as they were, I wasn't going to have a chance to apologize.

Just as I was about to reach Epona's room, a siren began to blare.

Does this mean the Royal Academy is under attack?

Attacking the school was insane. It was home to over one hundred mages. Even if some were inexperienced, that was still a massive force.

"...Well, I wouldn't be surprised if it's a force of monsters led by a demon."

An announcement echoed throughout the dormitory. It said to gather in the cafeteria right away. It also mentioned that a horde of monsters was headed for the academy. It wasn't just orcs this time, either. The incursion was comprised of many different species. This was shaping up to be a much larger battle than the last one.

"I knew those orcs were a trick."

I'd been suspicious of that orc attack right from the get-go. They'd behaved very strangely, and it'd led me to believe their real purpose had been reconnaissance. If that was correct, it didn't take much to guess what sort of information they'd been after.

The most probable answer was Epona's weaknesses. Their goal was to break the hero, and they'd achieved it. That's why those orcs had retreated when they did and why they were attacking the academy now.

Whoever was commanding the orcs must've deduced that Epona had trouble controlling her power and that it led to her hurting her allies in battle.

Epona was going to have a tough time fighting monsters in the academy. Undoubtedly, she was going to be afraid of hurting her peers.

"If we assume the goal of their attack is to weaken Epona, then we're in trouble. Even one hundred mages won't bother them if that's all they care about."

Monsters were beasts that acted on nothing more than instinct. Records showed that demons possessed higher intelligence, however. They could summon monsters and were very skilled commanders. Even so, I hadn't expected an attack quite this bold.

"Epona!"

After hearing the siren, the hero had rushed out of her room, and I called out to her. She started to say something, swallowed the words, then searched for something else to say.

"I'm going ahead. Please fight as far from me as possible."

She was still pushing me away.

"I'm sorry about before... Let's fight together again. I'll show you that I'm strong enough to handle it. You don't have to go it alone."

I didn't want to be a burden to her anymore.

Epona ran off without turning around to face me.

I'd said what I'd needed to. Now I had to see my promise done. Given the invasion, I definitely had the chance.

The army of monsters was drawing ever nearer, and the academy was understandably in an uproar.

Nearly all the students had gathered in the dining hall. The only ones not there were Epona and the top upperclassmen. One of the most prominent teams was already moving to intercept.

A professor went up on stage and began to speak.

"Everyone, I have gathered you all here for one reason. A force of monsters is currently targeting this academy. Hundreds of enemies are approaching from every way but the south, and their numbers are still increasing. It is a mixed force of orcs and goblins... There is almost certainly a demon among them."

That much was obvious. Monsters couldn't teleport, after all. Only the presence of a high-ranking demon capable of producing and commanding the creatures could explain the sudden appearance of an army.

"We have requested a dispatch of knights from the Royal Order, but it will take them at least half a day to get here. Unfortunately, our foes are nearly at our gates. This means we'll have to do what we can with our current personnel."

Help arriving in twelve hours was wishful thinking. The academy was already a stronghold and usually served the role of dispatching military strength. What's more, if the school was under siege, then the royal capital was likely in danger as well. It seemed highly unlikely that any help would be coming for us when the kingdom's rulers could be in peril.

"Students, steel yourselves. There is nowhere to run. This will be an all-out battle with no escape. Those who don't have the strength to engage, find a different way to contribute. We can't win unless everyone gives their all."

A silence hung over the dining hall. Many of the first-years were trembling. It was hard to blame them, since they had suddenly been hurled into such a deadly situation.

The professor went on to explain that students were to act in groups. Each one would consist of five to ten underclassmen and one leading upperclassman.

The discovery of the demon was to be reported right away. Engaging with it was strictly forbidden. Only the hero was capable of killing one.

Groups were formed, and students gathered around their leaders—with a few exceptions.

"Unbelievable. We're the only ones who don't get the protection of an upperclassman," I said with a little laugh.

Unlike other teams, Dia, Tarte, Naoise, and I were operating as our usual group, minus Epona.

"Personally, I don't mind. The faculty probably feels they need to keep the most capable students together, and I think it'll be easier this way," replied Naoise. He was half bluffing with that statement. He'd lost his confidence in the battle the other day, and it was clearly still troubling him.

The upperclassmen had already received their orders. After relaying the instructions to their charges, they moved out.

My group was the only one left in the dining hall. No one had given us our assignment yet.

A professor walked up to us.

"I have a special mission for the four of you. I couldn't say this in front of the regular students, but our defeat will be certain if this becomes a war of attrition. That means the hero is our only hope."

Epona was an untiring machine of slaughter, but she could only be in one place at a time. Our enemies were marching on our door from every direction but the south, where the capital lay. There was undoubtedly no end to the monsters' reinforcements. At best, an ordinary student could only keep up the fight for a few hours. Any group defending the academy without Epona's help was sure to fall.

None of this was a coincidence. The demon had crafted its strategy to ensure this would happen.

"We only see one way to achieve victory. Before our defenses fail, the demon must be located, and the hero must kill it. As such, your mission is to find the demon," the professor declared.

It was our only option. Stopping the demon would halt the supply of monsters.

I looked to Dia, Tarte, and Naoise, and we all nodded in acceptance.

"Understood. Professor, we will defend the academy and make finding the demon our number one priority," I said.

"I'm counting on you."

That team made entirely of upper-level students had probably been given the same mission.

We were stationed on the eastern side. Epona was defending the north. That was where most of the monsters were approaching. The rest of the academy's strength had been divided evenly between the other two directions.

No enemies were approaching from the south, likely because the demon knew the royal capital would dispatch troops if they pressed in from that direction.

The capital wasn't going to risk sending help when it needed to defend itself. Any hostile force between it and the academy could spur its knights into action, however. If the demons understood that much, it was clear they had a firm grasp of human thinking.

Two lines of defense had been established on the eastern side.

The first sat a reasonable distance ahead of the second and consisted only of upper-level students fighting furiously. They were skilled combatants, clearly at a level where they could've entered the Royal Order.

The senior students weren't worrying about any monsters that managed to get by them. Instead, they focused on preserving their physical and mental stamina by trying not to overexert themselves. Any foes that broke past were dealt with by the second line of defense. It was comprised of younger students under the command of older ones.

They were performing very well in that formation. The upperclassmen were making great use of the inexperienced lowerclassmen, giving clear orders and only asking them to do things they were capable of.

"Wow, the senior students really are so reliable," said an impressed Dia as she fired spells from behind the second line.

The upperclassmen weren't just giving orders; they were providing support when necessary, too.

Dia, Tarte, Naoise, and I were fighting on the second line. After observing the situation, I had a pretty good idea of what was going on.

We should go ahead and move.

"Naoise, Dia, Tarte, let's move up to the front line. We're going to look for the demon using the method we discussed earlier," I declared.

To pinpoint the location of the demon, we had to get to the front of the battle. That meant we'd be in greater danger, however.

"Okay, let's go," said Tarte.

"We need to do our part to help Epona," responded Dia.

"I'd look like quite the cad if I backed down after hearing Dia and Tarte say such things. I'll go, too... Following you seems like the best option anyway," Naoise agreed.

These are reliable companions. With them by my side, fighting will be no problem.

Things were raging up on the front lines.

...These monsters are even stronger than the orcs from last time.

I used mana to enhance my physical strength. I usually increased my power to a level that matched a regular mage, but this time I pushed it to the very limits of what an average mage should've been capable of.

"Tarte, have you mastered both eyes yet?" I asked.

"Of course. I won't fail like I did before. How about you, Lady Dia?"

"...I'm doing okay, too. I have them under control."

I'd been worried about the side effects of their Tuatha Dé

eyes. But Tarte had adapted to them, and Dia was an expert at mana control. I had no real cause for concern.

The four of us fought without any problems, even at the forefront of the battle. We weren't any less skilled than the upperclassmen. If anything, we were better.

Our joining with the older students immediately shifted the battle's tide on the eastern side to our favor. Many of our seniors turned to us and offered praise.

"I'd heard there were some real standouts among the first-years. You guys are terrific. Keep it up!"

"Thank you. Your support makes fighting a breeze," I answered.

"Ha-ha-ha, protecting younger students is the duty of an upperclassman. But can you really keep fighting at that pace?"

As he said, my group was fighting with all our might. We weren't pacing ourselves at all.

"Preserving our strength isn't our goal. Our mission is to pinpoint the location of the demon, and we're doing what we need to do to accomplish that," I explained.

"So you're hunting the leader... Hey, Granz, Bachal, Reina. Fight full strength for five minutes to help out these underclassmen! Given the current flow and momentum of the enemy, it will probably take another ten minutes."

"Roger."

"I'd thought about searching for the demon, too, but I never would've thought some younger students would be the ones to do it."

"You guys are impressive for a group of first-years. Leave this to us."

The upperclassmen stopped holding back and began to rip into the monsters with incredible force.

I'd barely said anything, and they'd figured out my entire plan. They truly were the best the academy had to offer.

Two hours passed, and the battle didn't show any signs of slowing down.

The situation had been getting steadily worse all the while. Injuries were starting to pile up. The wounded would retreat from the battle, but that only put a more significant burden on those still fighting, which meant more casualties. No one could afford to make a single mistake or take a moment to rest.

The enemy was too strong, and their numbers were also great. Until we found the demon and alerted Epona to its location, we didn't stand a chance of winning.

We can't put it off any longer. The academy is lost unless we act now.

I'd already ordered Dia and Tarte to fight without holding back. I was also using my Rapid Recovery to kill monsters at a fast rate. That was part of the plan to locate the demon.

Wherever it was, the creature was producing a steady stream of monsters. Killing them wasn't going to reduce their numbers. But thinking about this situation logically, what we were doing was the best way to pinpoint its location.

There was a good chance there was only one demon producing monsters. Any creatures it summoned were marching toward the academy from the demon's location. We merely had to follow the path of monsters to find the one in charge.

I'd been searching for that course while fighting.

The enemy wasn't stupid. They were taking precautions to conceal their location. To draw them out, I decided to create a situation that would force the demon to make a large number of monsters quickly. As such, my team was devoting itself to slaying as many orcs and goblins as we could.

My plan paid off almost immediately. Our target was summoning up new troops faster than they could cover their tracks. The road to the demon was now clear.

"Tarte, Dia, Naoise. I'm going to seek out the demon. Once I find it, I'll send up the signal. You three stay here and support the front line," I instructed.

"No, you can't go alone, my lord. It's too dangerous," protested Tarte.

"I can only accomplish this alone. Tracking the enemy requires the skill of my primary profession," I stated.

To find the demon, I would have to charge headfirst into the opposing army and slip behind enemy lines. Naturally, fighting through every monster on the way would've been impossible.

My experience as an assassin told me it was better that I took on this challenge alone.

"I can't believe I'm getting left behind again, but I'll protect the academy so you have somewhere to return to, my lord," Tarte agreed.

"I'll be angry if you come back hurt," Dia chided.

"You can count on me. By the way, I know this isn't the best time, but could you both kiss me for good luck? It turns out I'm feeling a little scared at the thought of charging into their army," I said.

"Yes, of course."

"You're hopeless, Lugh."

I kissed both Tarte and Dia, replenishing their mana in the process.

Being nervous had just been an excuse. The two girls had been pushing themselves very hard and had exhausted much of their magical power. A few pecks disguised as gestures of good fortune were all it took to bring them back to full capacity.

I admittedly felt strange kissing in the middle of a battlefield, but it was preferable to leaving Tarte and Dia low on mana.

"All right, I'm off."

"Good luck!"

"When you come back, let's have a normal kiss, okay?"

I smiled at the girls, then took a deep breath and took off at a run. I hurried forward into the enemy army, darting between the monsters.

Suddenly, I found myself struck by a sense of curiosity.

I wonder what sort of creature the demon is.

Following the path that new groups of monsters were traveling, I closed in on my quarry. Using the blood of felled orcs and goblins, I disguised my scent and kept as far out of sight as possible without losing the trail.

My approach was both daring and cautious. Getting caught now would've put me in the direst situation imaginable. Catching the eye of even a single monster meant dealing with an endless stream of them that would surely overwhelm me.

It was a terrifying thought.

After running for about three kilometers, I finally found it.

The demon resembled an orc but possessed a few distinguishing features. It was wearing armor made from a magical beast's skin, and its body was riddled with old scars. Its white hair and long beard gave it the appearance of a grizzled veteran who'd seen many battles.

Most startling was its detached jaw. Orcs and goblins were crawling from its gaping mouth. It was a grotesque sight, to say the least.

"That is really unpleasant to look at."

Evidently, this was the method by which the demon was creating new monsters.

I pulled a signal flare out of my pouch. It was a special item given to those who'd been tasked with finding the enemy army's leader.

I lit the fuse. The end of the thing flew upward and exploded with red light. It quite resembled a firework.

That will be visible from kilometers away. Epona should be here soon.

The problem was…

"I suppose this was bound to happen."

Every orc and goblin in my vicinity was bearing down on me now.

The flare alerted the hero to this location, but it also broadcasted my site to the enemy. I could've stayed safe by launching the signal from farther away, but that would've meant a less accurate beacon.

To make matters worse, I couldn't run. If this demonic, grizzled orc moved, then this all would've been for naught. I had no choice but to stay and watch it.

The agile goblins closed in on me by swinging like monkeys from the branches of surrounding trees. When the first one leaped at me, I threw a knife at its forehead, piercing through it and two others and knocking them all out of the air.

Thankfully, the surrounding forest limited the giant orcs' maneuverability. That afforded me enough time for an incantation.

"Firestorm!"

The flames of my spell burned right through the orcs' thick hides. I'd trapped all of the heat inside the storm by increasing the spell's precision, creating a cage to prevent any flames from escaping.

Two more orcs crumpled into smoldering piles.

Unfortunately…

"It's like a drop in the ocean."

There were still hundreds of monsters. Killing a few of them at a time wasn't going to accomplish anything.

Closing my eyes, I retrieved a flash grenade and threw it at my feet.

The world was bathed in white. I used that moment to run and hide.

While the orcs and goblins tried to search for me, it didn't seem like they were very good at sniffing out concealed opponents.

...All right, I'll hide right here until the great hero arrives.

I moved from one obscured spot to the next, keeping an eye on the demon all the while. My discovery seemed unlikely.

Something was odd, however. The demon appeared intelligent. It should've understood that my flare had been a signal for the hero. Curiously, it didn't seem to care, though. I had to observe it carefully. The creature was definitely up to something.

As I watched, I realized monsters were returning from the front lines.

I looked closely and realized those orcs that'd come from the forefront were carrying something. It appeared to be a big sack, and whatever was inside it was occasionally moving.

On the demon's order, the monsters opened the sack, revealing a group of students who'd been paralyzed by some sort of poison.

"So that's what they're planning."

Orcs already could increase their numbers by kidnapping females and impregnating them. The demon had used that instinct to make them collect students...to use as shields.

This was how the demon intended to exploit Epona's weakness. It was a strategy built to capitalize on Epona's fear of harming her allies.

Even after being discovered, the demon hadn't retreated because it wanted to face the hero.

...This is bad. Can I save the students before Epona gets here?

"If there were one or two students, I'd be able to pull it off. But twenty-three of them..."

It was impossible. Killing those orcs surrounding the hostages was simple enough, but I couldn't grab over twenty people and carry them out.

A sudden explosion caught my attention.

"I finally found you—my enemy. I will kill you and fulfill my duty. I'll become a real hero. I'll protect the Alvanian Kingdom just like I promised Mireille I would."

Epona had left a path of destruction in her wake. Everything around her had been mowed down. Craters burst into the earth with each of her steps. Her strength was as unbelievable as ever.

The horde of orcs laughed, and the orc that looked like a war veteran—the demon—walked forward.

"The hero is still but a child, green and unskilled."

"You're not wrong, but that won't stop me from accomplishing what I've come here to do."

"Oh-hooo, you *are* brave. I'd give you my name as a reward for making it this far, but a human wouldn't be able to comprehend it. I suppose I'll settle for a rough translation. I am General Orc, the most powerful orc of all."

It seemed a fitting name for a leader of orcs and goblins.

"I'm Epona, the hero."

"Oh-ho-hooo. Epona. I will remember it. Let's have ourselves some fun, hero. I was hoping to give my side an advantage before everyone else wakes up."

General Orc's words were nonchalant, but they undoubtedly held some significance.

What's he playing at? While I was considering that question, the battle began.

The horde of burly orcs rushed at Epona.

Even such gigantic creatures were no match for the hero. Epona swung an arm as if swatting away a fly in annoyance. The motion spilled the innards of several orcs at once. Then she used a simple blast of raw mana to send everything around her flying in all directions.

Her strength was overwhelming. For some reason, however, General Orc began to laugh and summon more monsters.

Epona's movements grew clumsy. The orcs brought out the kidnapped students to use as shields. They'd tied the students to their hideous stomachs.

"You coward!" Epona exclaimed.

"This is strategy. Monsters can't afford to fight fair against the hero, you know," General Orc said with raucous delight.

Epona continued to fight, taking care to avoid injuring our captured classmates.

While Epona was an unskilled fighter—both due to her inexperience and her absurd strength—her strong defenses usually made up for that.

"Hmm, I thought you'd understand this without me having to spell it out, but...you seem like you don't get it. Stop fighting, or else."

General Orc gave a signal, and an orc bit off a male student's head, killing him.

Epona ground her teeth and glared at the demon, but she didn't stop fighting.

"Hmm, the hero sheds no tears."

"If I lose, you'll kill them anyway."

I'd thought for sure the tender and meek Epona would've surrendered after seeing something so gruesome, but she grasped the reality of the situation quite clearly. She was right in thinking the students were dead if she gave herself up. It was better not to concern herself with the hostages.

She didn't look at all like the person who'd been wracked with guilt after hurting Tarte in the last battle. It wasn't her allies getting hurt that Epona found so unpleasant. It was them dying by her hand that she despised.

"Gah-ha-ha-ha-ha-ha-ha, yes, yes, yes! It seems like you're not such a fool after all. But why are your movements becoming so clumsy?" General Orc needled.

The orcs with hostages tied to them moved forward.

Epona fought awkwardly as she tried to avoid the captives.

Epona's great fear only comes from killing people herself.

Her expression betrayed her thoughts to me. Epona was hoping the monsters would kill the hostages so she could go all out.

The longer the fight raged on, the stranger Epona's behavior became. Every step was less graceful than the last. Her eyes were shining, and a smirk was spreading across her face. I could see her mana increasing, and her muscles were bulging.

She's drunk on blood and battle.

"YOU'RE SOOOO ANNOOOOYYYIIIIIIING!"

Epona swung her fist as hard as she could, piercing through both an orc and a hostage.

"NOOOOOOOOOOOOOOO! I—I DID IT AGAIN!"

After Epona's scream, the orcs charged at her, brazenly thrusting the hostages forward. Instinctively, she counterattacked, killing more students.

Epona's face went pale, and she began to shake.

…She has some skill that causes her to lose reason when fighting, and the shock of killing people brings her out of it.

Epona vomited before collapsing to the ground. It was clear she couldn't continue fighting.

"There's no way I can just sit back and watch," I said.

Saving the hostages on my own would've been impossible. However, Epona's presence made it possible. I hadn't just been idly watching. I'd been working on a plan and waiting for the best time to leap in and save the captives.

The time had come for me to join Epona. I'd already broken my promise once, and I wasn't about to do it again. I still had to apologize to her, after all.

Hurriedly, I began an incantation.

"Arrange!"

Twenty guns popped out from the Leather Crane Bag. It was enough firepower to save the remaining hostages and then some. I set them in midair using magnetism from earth magic.

After careful research on the Leather Crane Bag, I'd discovered how to draw out the exact quantity of the items I wanted from its depths.

I'd selected guns over cannons so as not to harm the captives.

The barrels were filled with Fahr Stones crushed down into a powder. The amount of force packed into a single rifle required delicate adjustment. Even the slightest error in volume risked causing an explosion when fired.

Rifles were superior to heavy armaments when it came to accuracy and maneuverability. Their smaller firing force also meant lower recoil, which enabled me to use them while they were hovering instead of rooting them to the ground.

They were the perfect choice for my current situation.

"Aim!"

Using magnetism, I leveled each of the barrels at their respective targets.

Aiming twenty rifles at once would've been impossible for

an ordinary mage. Rapid Recovery and Limitless Growth had allowed my brain to become capable of more than any regular person, so it was no problem for me.

The guns locked onto their targets, accounting for environmental factors.

"Rifle Volley!"

After pouring mana into it, the Fahr Stone powder in each barrel reached its critical point, causing the guns to fire. Every shot blasted off the head of one of the orcs with a hostage tied to it.

It was an extremely powerful and precise attack that not even the hero could pull off.

Blood and gray matter splattered everywhere. The now-headless orcs collapsed one after another.

I'd also launched a bullet at General Orc's head, thinking I might get lucky. While it struck his head, that's all it did. He was as tough as you would've expected a demon to be.

"Epona! Gather the hostages!" I yelled. It was impossible for me to carry all the hostages and escape, but I could definitely handle killing orcs while Epona gathered up our classmates and fled.

"Lugh?"

"Quickly!"

Still pale, Epona collected all of the hostages. The orcs tried to get to them first, but Epona was significantly swifter.

With them out of the way, she would be able to fight without any issues.

The cost of saving them had been exposing one of my secret attacks in front of my assassination target, but it was a fair trade. It'd been the only way to save Epona and the hostages.

"Oh-ho-hooo, this is unexpected. You're the boy who raised

the signal flare. You've ruined my plan. But ah well. On to the next one. This is checkmate. Hoh-hoh-hoh."

General Orc turned around and took off running, moving at an unbelievable speed considering his sluggish appearance. Then, as if to ensure their leader got away, the remaining orcs charged at us.

...*Everything up to this point suggested their goal was to kill Epona. What are they planning?*

The time for pondering was later. I had monsters to slay.

"Epona, what are you doing? Finish off these small fries and go after the demon. As long as he is alive, the enemies will keep coming," I insisted.

"Y-yeah, I know. I know that, but..."

Epona tried to move forward but only vomited again. She looked at the rescued hostages. Evidently, she was still recovering from having killed a few.

...*It looks like I won't be able to rely on her.*

"Okay, then rest right there. I'll kill these orcs," I declared.

"UGAAAAAAAA!"

"GROOOOOOOUUUGGHR!"

Sixty guns emerged from my bag. That was the maximum I was capable of controlling at once. I prepared another Rifle Volley.

After revealing this technique to the hero, there was no reason to hold back on it anymore.

It only took me a few minutes to wipe out all of the orcs. However, we'd completely lost sight of General Orc.

"I had no idea you were this powerful," remarked Epona with a tired expression on her face.

"...More importantly, we've lost sight of the demon. I'm going to see if I can find him," I replied.

I strengthened my Tuatha Dé eyes to their limit and climbed the tallest tree I could find. It didn't take long to spot where General Orc had scurried off to.

He said he had a follow-up plan... I see. So that's what he meant.

Unconsciously, I bit my lip at the sight of it.

"They're gathering their scattered strength into one spot. I can't believe how many there are."

Fearing being wiped out by the hero, the monsters had abandoned a three-pronged strategy and were instead gathering together as one force. Together, they marched slowly toward the academy with General Orc at the center of it all.

In response, the academy was gathering what remained of its forces to meet the impending attack.

In less than ten minutes, things were going to descend into an all-out battle. And that's exactly what the demon wanted. General Orc knew Epona couldn't handle harming her compatriots and aimed to create a chaotic brawl where that would be unavoidable.

I conveyed the situation to Epona.

"Go, Epona. If you don't, everyone in the academy will be killed."

Even after hearing that, Epona still didn't move.

I pulled her by the hand, but she knocked mine aside.

"I can't do it. I'll only hurt more people in a fight like that, and I won't be able to battle properly. I'll get more and more heated, I'll lose myself, and I'll go blind to my surroundings and kill again. Just like I killed Mireille!! I'll kill everyone, even you, Lugh!"

Epona sank to the ground.

"Did you forget my promise? I won't die. And if you should lose yourself, I'll stop you."

"That's impossible. You can't stop me, Lugh. You didn't last time, did you? Nobody can stop me. I don't want to kill anymore," Epona whimpered, smiling at me through tears.

…*That's right. I did fail last time.* I'd said I would stop Epona, but then I was unable to, and Tarte got hurt. I gathered my thoughts with a deep breath and readied myself.

At this rate, our school was going to be overwhelmed. Tarte, Dia, and all my classmates would be killed. The hero was our only hope of victory.

But Epona couldn't get up. No matter what I said, she wasn't going to stand.

If words aren't enough, I'll show her with actions and sincerity.

"Can you give me one more chance? This time, I will keep my promise. To tell the truth, I've been holding back my real strength. Just watch. I'll show you that I am strong enough to stop you." With that, I took off running.

I strengthened myself to the max.

Using my near-limitless mana, I discharged as much as I could at once. My body housed at least ten times the magical power of a regular mage, and I was using all of it to boost my strength.

I can't be reluctant to show my full strength anymore.

"Amazing, so this is Lugh's power," muttered Epona. She had to understand now that my promise hadn't been a bluff.

I still hadn't done enough for her to trust me, though. I was going to use my full strength to wipe out the orcs. Even if killing the demon proved impossible, I wanted Epona to know I could handle the rest.

Hopefully, that would restore the hero's trust in me. If it did, she could take down the demon.

To protect Dia and Tarte and to keep the promise I'd made to my friend Epona, I was ready to play every card in my arsenal. It didn't matter if the hero knew all my tricks. I would just make new ones.

I ran toward the army of monsters, Epona following behind me silently. She wanted to make sure I could keep my oath.

In the middle of my sprint, I began an incantation.

Engaging such an enormous army head-on was suicide. That's why I was going to use the most destructive magic I had.

The rods from God—Gungnir.

Gungnir's biggest weakness was that it took ten minutes to land because it had to free-fall from one thousand kilometers up in the air. That long timer made precise aiming impossible. Unless the target was someone as powerful as the hero, a direct hit wasn't really required.

I released a tungsten spear into the sky in preparation.

My inexhaustible supply of mana was enough to allow me to fire multiple spears. I continued to launch god spears into the air as I ran toward the enemy army.

I came to a stop about four hundred fifty meters away. Any closer than that, and I risked getting caught in my own attack.

The orcs and goblins continued their advance on the academy, unaware of my plan.

While it was risky, I needed to attract their attention toward me. If the monsters pressed any closer to the school, my attack could harm those defending it.

This is the most power I can wield without harming my allies.

"I won't hold back!"

I pulled a Fahr Stone out of my pouch and filled it to its critical point. I produced a bow and some arrows with magic, attached the Fahr Stone to one shaft, and fired.

"Take that!"

I pulled hard on the tough bowstring explicitly made for use in my physically enhanced state and launched the Fahr Stone arrow over four hundred fifty meters. It landed in front of the advancing monsters and exploded.

The Fahr Stone was filled with 70 percent fire mana, 20 percent wind mana, and 10 percent earth mana. After it detonated, flames burst forth, wind fanned the fire, and iron shrapnel flew in all directions.

Dozens of orcs and goblins were slaughtered. Any explosion brought about by mana equivalent to that of three hundred ordinary mages combined was going to cause some real damage.

Remaining in place, I fired one Fahr Stone after another. All of them were aimed at the enemy's front line, just like the first one.

Shots toward the center of the army would've killed more monsters, but my goal was to slow their advance, not wipe them out. The loud bursts were also a warning for everyone at the academy to stay back. If they got any closer, they were going to die to Gungnir.

Just as I'd intended, the monsters and the academy forces stopped in their tracks. While crying out in strange voices, the orcs and goblins turned toward the source of all this destruction—me.

I'd used up all of the Fahr Stones in my pouch. I needed to

replenish them with more from my Leather Crane Bag. More importantly, however, the time for my trump card had arrived.

"Eat this! The rods from God... *Gungnir!*"

A spear sped down from the heavens. Upon landing, it tore apart the earth, creating a radial impact crater with a bottom deeper than could be seen with the naked eye. A tsunami of dirt poured out from the point of collision.

If an object with a mass of one hundred kilograms fell from a height of one thousand kilometers in the sky, it would accelerate to a speed of four thousand kilometers per second, making it the ultimate projectile.

America had once attempted to develop such a weapon as a successor to the nuclear bomb. I'd successfully realized that theory using my magic. It was my most potent killing move.

Not even scraps remained of any monster caught within a one-hundred-meter radius of the spear. Even those orcs and goblins farther away were swept up by the shock wave and crushed beneath waves of sediment.

And that was only the first blow. Down came a second, third, fourth, and the rest of the remaining nine god spears I'd fired into the sky. The impact points had been calculated such that none of the monsters would be able to escape.

"So this is Lugh's true strength. Not even I can do anything like that," Epona said from behind me. I even sensed some fear in her voice.

Now there's something to brag about. Not just anyone could've gotten the hero to say something like that.

Unfortunately, it'd taken exposing the most powerful attack I had to do it. Everything I revealed was only going to make assassinating Epona more difficult in the future.

There'd been no other choice, though. I had to protect those dear to me, and I was still hopeful I could find a way to save the world without killing Epona.

I could handle the small fries myself. But demons were another story. If Epona didn't recover, the world was doomed. I wanted to safeguard Dia, Tarte, and this academy.

"How in the world did those monsters survive that...?"

When the aftermath of Gungnir cleared, I spied eight figures slowly clawing their way out of the dirt. All it took was a look to know they were superior to average orcs.

These might be the rumored Elite Monsters. Considering we hadn't seen them until now, it seemed like General Orc had been saving them as a last-ditch effort. Only a direct hit from Gungnir could've killed them.

I'd been expecting as much, however.

I took out my Leather Crane Bag.

"Arrange!"

From its depths, I called up multiple giant cannons.

These cannons made the guns I'd used to rescue the hostages look like toys. Their 120 mm barrels were the size of tank artillery, and the pedestals they were sitting on were spiked into the ground. Rather than Fahr Stones broken into powder to lessen their force, the massive cannons were filled with full-size Fahr Stones, each containing the mana of three hundred ordinary mages.

As thick as it was, my prototype cannon couldn't handle the explosions of full-size Fahr Stones. But these new models were different. I'd increased the thickness, improved the alloy, and used some spells to strengthen them. They were durable weapons capable of enduring Fahr Stone explosions.

The cannons took time to produce, but with the Leather Crane Bag, I could prepare them beforehand and carry them around, enabling me to use them in battle.

"*Aim!*"

At my magical command, my battery leveled its barrels at the eight surviving Elite Monsters.

The dim-witted orcs faced me. As if confident they were impervious, they didn't try to dodge.

...It does make sense that they would have that level of confidence in their defense. They survived Gungnir, but only because they weren't hit dead-on. They're overestimating themselves.

"*Cannon Volley!*"

The cannons fired simultaneously, using entire Fahr Stones as gunpowder. In other words, three hundred mages' worth of mana was converted directly into a destructive force. Rather than a bomb, that energy was concentrated into individual cannon shells. The area of effect was slimmer than Gungnir, but cannons were more suited for picking off a few targets anyway.

Among my easy-to-use spells, this one boasted the most force. The proof of that was right before our eyes.

Each of the eight Elite Monsters was pierced through its abdomen, and the force of the impact ripped them all to shreds.

In mere moments, they were dead. I alone had eradicated an entire army that had caused terrible pain and suffering for the academy.

I turned around and smiled at Epona.

"Certain circumstances had forced me to conceal my strength previously, but this is the real me. Allow me to make the promise from that day one more time. You won't kill me. If you start to rampage, I will use my full strength to stop you. Do you trust me?"

Epona opened her mouth to reply.

Then...I leaped backward as far as I could.

A giant metal club swung down onto the spot where I'd been standing. General Orc was the one wielding it.

Despite his fearsome size and strength, he'd managed to hide his presence, dive into the dirt, and travel underground to take me by surprise. He may have looked like an orc, but he was quite the clever foe.

"Aww, I thought I was going to kill you there. Do you ever let your guard down, you little brat?"

"You could learn a thing or two from me in that regard."

Assassins never let their guard down. General Orc could try to hide as much as he liked, but my eyes could see mana. I'd spotted him slinking toward me from below the earth. I'd even had time to prepare a counterattack.

The moment I dodged his metal club, I threw a Fahr Stone at its critical point into his dumb, gaping mouth, where it promptly exploded.

No matter how strong this demon was, he couldn't endure the force of a Fahr Stone detonating inside his head unharmed.

General Orc's head was blasted off his shoulders.

However...

"You almost got me there. If you'd been the hero instead of that pathetic female, you probably would've killed me. But unfortunately for you, you're just a lowly human."

His head regenerated an instant after I'd blown it up.

It wasn't just some cheap healing factor; there was something unusual about it. Whatever it was, it seemed only the hero could kill a demon.

Demons had bodies, but their own essences sustained them.

Their physical forms could regenerate endlessly unless that energy was snuffed out. Only Epona was capable of such a feat.

"Epona, you need to fight! Do you still not trust me after everything I just showed you?" I asked.

"But I…"

"You're acting quite calm for being in the middle of a battle. You're going to regret that."

With the characteristic strength of an orc, General Orc began to swing his tree-trunk-sized club around.

The speed of his attacks defied common sense, and despite being able to see them, I could only barely dodge them.

While General Orc's strikes appeared crude, nothing could've been further from the truth. Despite the excessive force of the demon's downward swings, he was still able to stop in the middle of them and change his club's direction. Such an ability made General Orc's movements challenging to predict and nerve-racking to deal with.

I would've been hit long ago if I was only relying on my own power. The only reason I was able to evade was that I'd taken a drug to remove the limiter on my brain. My physical capabilities had been boosted by a combination of a particular chemical and a mana supply that was a thousand times as much as the average person.

That medicine was yet another one of the secrets I'd been hoping to save for the hero.

I'm not going to be able to push myself like this for much longer.

General Orc's club landed right at my feet. I'd skirted death, but the rush of air knocked me backward. In response, I hurled an envenomed titanium knife, and it stuck into the demon's thigh.

"Ooh, I didn't think there was a poison that could render me immobile. But all I have to do is remove the affected flesh. Like so."

General Orc tore off his leg. A new one quickly sprouted in its place, and the demon charged at me.

This is getting bad. Rapid Recovery kept me from being physically exhausted, but I didn't know how long my concentration was going to last.

I wasn't fighting to defeat General Orc. I was fighting to gain Epona's trust.

Before I got beaten to a pulp, I had to show the hero I was strong so that she'd choose to fight.

This isn't going to be easy.

I'd routed an army of hundreds of monsters, and now there was only one left. Unfortunately, it was a battle I couldn't win.

"You are clearly not a knight, boy. You don't fight by the rules, and you show no mercy. This is fun. I wonder how you'll kill me this time."

With pure joy on his face, General Orc came at me again.

I'd been changing up my killing method throughout the battle. Thus far, I should've slain General Orc ten times. I'd cut him, beaten him, strangled him, stabbed him, punched him, poisoned him, bombed him, crushed him, burned him, and shot him.

What enabled me to kill him so many different ways was the Leather Crane Bag Maha had acquired for me. Not a single one of the demon's deaths had stuck, however. Each time, he immediately revived and chased after me as though nothing had happened. I was running out of techniques.

"Wind Cage!"

I performed an original incantation of mine, and the spell manifested. It allowed me to manipulate the air to create a cage around my target. While that didn't sound too impressive, it was quite problematic for the one trapped within.

I filled the cage with carbon dioxide. If a person were placed into a closed space filled with nothing but carbon dioxide, all of the oxygen in their body would be immediately released, causing instant suffocation.

This was yet another tactic I'd devised to kill the hero. No matter how strong Epona was, she needed to breathe like any other human. That meant she'd die if denied oxygen. Hopefully, the same was true of demons.

General Orc's eyes rolled into the back of his head, and he died.

I jumped back to gain distance and catch my breath. I'd been giving everything I had for a while now, even going so far as to take a drug to remove my brain's natural limits. I'd expended a significant amount of stamina and mana, and I was sporting quite a few injuries as well.

Rapid Recovery raised my skill level and multiplied my recovery rate by one hundred twenty, but that didn't mean I was a limitless font of energy. In one second, I regained what anyone else would've in one hundred twenty seconds. If I expended stamina faster than I could recover, I'd collapse.

For a while now, I'd been fighting at a rate that outpaced my Rapid Recovery.

"That was a first. I've never died without even understanding how it happened. But you're never going to be able to finish me off."

Unsurprisingly, General Orc returned to life. I'd been observing him very carefully throughout our struggle.

"...Well, if that's what you think, then come at me," I beckoned with a thin smile.

I'd been intentionally testing a variety of killing methods on him. Each time, I carefully studied the way he resurrected by using my Tuatha Dé eyes. My hope was that I'd discover the mechanism behind his immortality after watching the fluctuations in his mana with each different death.

Demonology books explained a demon's healing factor in abstract terms, like "reincarnation brought about by the creature's power of existence." I didn't intend to take such vague scripture at face value. There had to be some sort of quantifiable rule. If I could figure it out, then I could kill General Orc.

...*I really don't want to give up.* I disliked the idea of dying simply because Epona never chose to do anything. That's why I'd been working on my own path to victory. I even had a contingency strategy if I genuinely couldn't take down General Orc.

At this pace, I was only going to be able to fight for fifty more seconds. A moment's hesitation meant certain doom.

It looked like I only had one thing left that I could do—retreat while I still had the strength to do so, then hide and recover. After that, I'd return to the academy, gather Dia and Tarte, and escape. If I enacted that option within the next twenty seconds, I was sure I could pull it off.

Ten more seconds...

"You look like you're up to something. You'd better make this fun!"

Looking every bit the predator, General Orc brought his metal club down at me as if it were the only thing he knew how to do.

My time's up. I'll dodge this and run.

I read the trajectory of the club, but I ended up not needing to dodge it.

"Lugh, you've made your strength clear." Epona caught the demon's weapon. No matter how hard he tried, General Orc couldn't even get it to budge. "You are strong. You still can't stop me...but you might be able to kill me. Promise me one thing. If

I ever become a monster, kill me. If you promise me that, I'll be able to fight."

I grinned. That was exactly what I'd been planning to do from the start.

Until there was no other course of action left but to slay Epona, I had vowed to be her friend. On that day in the cemetery, I'd chosen to find a way to save the world without ending her life.

"You think you can have a chat in front of me?!"

General Orc summoned another metal club from out of nowhere and swung it down. It collided with Epona's head and immediately shattered.

"You're getting on my nerves."

Epona grabbed General Orc's arm and hurled him into a stone wall.

A crimson haze surrounded Epona.

I know this skill. It was the S-Rank skill Berserk. Setanta, the man in Soigel who I'd suspected of being the hero, had used it.

A man using Berserk grew horns and had their muscles swell. A woman using the skill was enveloped in a fiery aura.

"Lugh, can you promise you'll kill me?" asked Epona, repressing the influence of Berserk, which could cause her to lose her mind at any second.

"I promise. If you ever become a monster, I'll put you down. I'll even let you in on a secret of mine. I am an assassin, so that kind of thing is my specialty," I admitted.

Epona smiled. A was an expression full of childlike innocence.

Because she decided to trust me, I decided to reveal my true identity to her as a friend.

"That puts me at ease."

Epona turned to face General Orc, who was slumped on the ground before the wall. She walked toward him slowly, step by step, gradually increasing her power along the way.

The red haze burned hotter and hotter. As Epona's infinite power rose, her face became increasingly twisted with insanity.

She clenched her fists tight.

"Wh-what is this power? Even for the hero, this level of strength should be... No way...you're not an imitation—you're the original."

There was panic on General Orc's face for the first time.

"Don't come near meeeeeeeeeeeeeeee!"

He opened his big mouth to spawn more orcs and goblins, made them rush at Epona, and then tried to flee.

However, the orcs and goblins didn't even slow Epona down for a second. The moment any made contact with Epona's aura, they vanished without a trace.

I doubt even the bullets from my Cannon Strike would be able to make it through that crimson glow. I'm not even sure Gungnir would make it.

Once Epona entered that state, there was no chance of killing her. I wouldn't even be able to touch her.

"I already can't contain myself... Kee-hee-hee-hee-hee, I'll crush you with everything I have."

Epona focused her power into her fist.

"STOPPPPPPPPPP!"

"AH-HA-HA-HA-HA-HA-HA! HA-HA-HA-HA-HA-HA!"

General Orc's scream was lost amid Epona's laughter.

Before Epona's all-out attack even made contact, General Orc disappeared utterly, and a red shock wave carved its way through the ground.

I flooded as much mana into my eyes as I could and observed. General Orc's body evaporated like water, and then a red jewel-like thing shattered, ending his existence.

I'd now seen how to kill a demon. After comparing it to the various ways I'd tried, I finally understood how it worked.

That red jewel was General Orc's true form, but of course, getting to it and destroying it was no easy task. The hero possessed some special characteristic that enabled her to reach it.

"Good thing Epona decided to throw her fist forward," I remarked.

If she'd struck the ground with that much force, it undoubtedly would've caused more destruction than Gungnir.

All right, time for my final job.

Epona was looking up at the sky with bloodshot eyes, roaring with laughter. I hit her with a Cannon Strike to the chin that knocked her unconscious.

"I promised I would kill her, but it looks like I didn't need to this time."

That was a close call. Epona had lost all sense of reason. If she'd been allowed to do as she pleased, I doubted the academy would've survived. That was why containing her power was so important.

Cannon Strike only got through because I'd hit Epona the moment after she'd released her heat haze during her all-out attack.

Even when she was not surrounded by that burning aura, the most my powerful Cannon Strike could do to the hero was knock her unconscious. It was ludicrous.

As strong as she was, I had the perfect opportunity to end her now that she was out cold.

I looked down at Epona. One strike to her vitals with Gungnir was likely all it would take to snuff out her life.

But I'd decided not to do that.

"Even if I don't attempt it, I've already proven I can kill her," I said to myself.

Knocking her out after she'd exhausted her power was all it took to get her defenseless. After that, it was just a matter of choosing which of my ace attacks to use. I'd made an important discovery today.

I picked Epona up and began to walk back to the academy. Before she woke up, I wanted to tell everyone she was the one who'd wiped out all the orcs. If it got out that I was capable of such a thing, it would undoubtedly cause me unnecessary trouble.

While carrying Epona on my back, I looked around at the devastation of the surrounding area. My god spears had altered the terrain significantly. This marked the first appearance of a demon in this era, and it had taken an incredible toll on the academy.

As the school came into view, I saw people running up to meet me.

Okay, how should I explain this?

After being questioned about what'd happened for an hour, I was released. I'd made Epona out to be the one who'd done everything.

No sooner had I left the visitation room than Dia and Tarte rushed over. They'd clearly been waiting. It was a relief to see them both safe.

"Welcome back, my lord."

"You really put on a show this time."

It sounded like they both realized it was all my doing.

"It was the first time I've been able to let loose like that in a while, so it felt good," I said.

"Is it really okay? You showed your true power in front of the hero," Tarte replied.

"Of course it's not okay," I answered.

"I knew it…"

If Epona had any measure of analytical skill, then she knew just about every major attack in my arsenal. The fight with General Orc had forced me to use them all. It was a huge loss.

"But I'm sure you don't regret it," Dia reasoned.

"Yeah, I wanted to protect this academy and the both of you. That is my number one priority. And besides, if you help me, Dia, I'm sure we can produce even more amazing magic," I stated.

I patted the girls on the heads, and they both leaned on me.

"What will happen to the academy?" Dia asked.

"It'll probably be closed temporarily," I explained.

The outer wall had crumbled, making the place unsuitable as a stronghold. There were many wounded; some had even died. I wouldn't have been surprised if the school shut down for good.

"That sucks. I really loved living here," Dia said with remorse.

"…Me too," I admitted.

There was nothing to be done about that now, though. Whatever happened next was up to the adults.

"For the time being, we should stop standing around. Let's go back. I'm hungry. With luck, they're distributing food somewhere," I said.

"Just in case they're not, I have some food for us. I've made a habit of preserving our leftovers and hiding them," Tarte revealed.

"Since when? I had no idea you were doing that sort of thing," Dia replied.

"Hee-hee-hee, it's because I grew up in a poor village. I know the pain of starvation well."

Tarte was probably the only noble servant who'd thought to do that. It brought a smile to my face.

We arrived at the dorm, which had luckily survived the battle. After I ate, I chose to take it easy for the rest of the day.

The following morning, all the students were gathered together for an assembly, where an academy shutdown was announced. Repairs would reportedly take two months, and we were to wait at our respective homes until they were complete. Summer vacation was two months long, so this absence was counted as that break instead.

I was glad they didn't have to close the academy.

To my surprise, noble families weren't upset about the danger their children had been in. Instead, the academy received adulation for wiping out a demon and its army so quickly after their appearance. Fighting monsters was the duty of mages, so that did make sense.

"We have a two-month break? That's quite a lot of free time," said Tarte.

"There are several things I've wanted to do recently. This is good timing," I responded.

Most urgently, I wanted to test a demon-slaying method I'd devised. I was also going to need an arsenal of killing moves. I hoped to accomplish both before returning to the academy.

Epona walked up to us with a timid look on her face. It was clear she wanted to apologize for something, but she did seem a bit more chipper.

"Sorry for waiting so long to express my gratitude... Thank you for stopping me."

"I did make a promise."

"Please stop me again the next time I get like that."

"I will. Even if it means killing you."

The promise I'd made to Epona and the reason I'd been sent to this world were one and the same. If there were no other way to stop the hero but killing her, I'd do it without a second thought. Until such a time, I would try my best to stop her from destroying everything without ending her life.

"All right, I'm gonna go," Epona declared.

"Are you returning to your hometown?" I asked.

"No, I'm going to be staying at a Royal Order base."

That was likely so she could be dispatched in the event of another demon attack.

"I suppose that means we're not going to see each other for a while," I observed.

"I'll miss you, Lugh. Good-bye."

"Yeah, until next time."

I watched Epona turn and leave.

"Tarte, Dia. Let's go home."

Knights arrived to transport students to the nearest town.

"Yes, my lord. After we get back, I'll make a feast using Tuatha Dé ingredients."

"I want to look back over the research documents I couldn't take to the academy."

I was going to work on getting stronger. I also needed to complete a method for killing demons.

It was more than just a desire to save Epona. The demons had to be stopped, or I'd lose everything dear to me. If that was inevitable, I at least wanted the comfort of knowing I'd done all I could. My pride refused to allow me to leave everything to the hero.

After our horse-drawn carriage arrived, we climbed in and began the journey home.

I opened my window and looked back at the academy.

"I will be back."

The school was growing very small in the distance. I'd only been there for a short while, but I'd had a lot of fun.

I'll return even more powerful.

Afterword

Thank you very much for reading *The World's Finest Assassin Gets Reincarnated in Another World as an Aristocrat*, Vol. 2. I am the author, Rui Tsukiyo.

In this second volume, we met the hero, the person whom the goddess tasked Lugh with killing.

I wonder what Lugh will do now that he's met the person he's supposed to assassinate!

The second volume has improved a lot since the web novel version. It's like an entirely different work. I hope you enjoyed it.

The third volume will be a bit more of a romantic comedy, and more of this world's secrets will be revealed as well!

Promotion

Kadokawa Sneaker Bunko will be putting out the sixth volume of my other series, *Redo of Healer*, on the same day. It's a revenge story that gets pretty lewd and harsh. If it sounds interesting, why not pick it up?

Thanks

To everyone who picked up this book, and to all the people involved in its creation, thank you very much!

The World's Finest Assassin Gets Reincarnated in Another World as an Aristocrat, Vol. 2

Congratulations on the release of the second volume!

Life at the academy began, and the hero made their appearance!

I'm so excited!! ゝ∠"

れい亜
(Reia)